The Honeysuckle Cafe

SOUTHERN CHARM
BOOK ONE

LILLY MIRREN

Cover design by Erin D'Ameron Hill.

Chapter One

Matilda Berry climbed out of the minivan at the Gold Coast Airport. Her sister, Stella, wouldn't come in, preferring to park the car at the Kiss 'N Drop. She gave her a breath-stealing hug before rushing back into the driver's seat with tears streaming down her cheeks.

Matilda watched her go with tear-blurred eyes and a wan smile. Stella always cried about everything. It was an endearing quality now they were adults. She hadn't liked it so much as kids, especially when it meant she'd get in trouble with their parents over some minor infraction.

Her heart ached. There was no turning back now. Did she have her passport? Nerves jolted up her neck. She patted her pocket. There it was, safe and sound. Pulse returned to normal. What about the ticket? Another jolt of nerves. No, that's right, it was all on her phone which was safely stowed in her carry on. She'd decided to leave from the much smaller airport because it was easier to navigate. There was a sparse crowd and only a few metres to get from the check-in to the gate.

The scent of salt lingered in the air. If only she could head to the beach and catch a few waves before she left. But there was no time. She was already checked in—had done that online on the drive down from Brisbane—and was ready to board her flight. The first leg was Los Angeles. Maybe she should've stopped there, seen the sights, visited Hollywood. But she wasn't quite ready to do all of that alone, and she had tunnel vision. She was eager to achieve her goal.

With a tug, she pulled her phone free from the backpack's pocket and stared at the screen. Seven missed calls from her boyfriend, or ex-boyfriend, she supposed. Was he an ex? It was hard to say. Cam had called her more in the days after their supposed breakup than he had in all the weeks preceding it. She'd answered the first few messages but after a while she'd grown irritated and ignored him for the most part.

After everything that'd happened between then, she needed some time to think. And she couldn't do that with him harassing her. She'd sent him a text explaining that and he hadn't tried to contact her since, until today. He knew she was leaving and probably wanted to say goodbye. But she was in no mood to be guilted into giving him sympathy. She was a little anxious about flying and needed to focus on getting to her flight on time.

She made her way through security and was soon at the gate. At a cafe close to the gate, she purchased a muffin that was nearly the size of her head and an enormous latte. Then, carrying them to the gate, she sat in one of the chairs near the window to watch the planes taxi to and from the terminal.

The hum of conversation, the clatter of cups on saucers, the announcements over the loudspeakers, it all blended together as her thoughts drifted away to another time and place.

She and Cam had driven to Double Island Point for some four-wheel driving, a swim in the pristine waters, and a picnic on the sand. It was a beautiful day. One she'd remember for a long time. They were falling in love, or at least she thought so. Their relationship was new and exciting—when every look, every touch, sent a tingle across her skin and up her spine.

She'd laid back on the towel, in the sand, and glanced up at the colourful beach umbrella overhead. It couldn't cut the glare though, so she reached for a pair of oversized, dark sunglasses and slipped them on. Her wet hair cooled her head, and her blue bikini looked bright against the brown of the towel and the pale golden sand.

"Do you ever think about having a family?" he'd asked, with a glance in her direction.

She smiled. "Sometimes."

"And?"

"I'd like one. Someday," she said. "If I meet the right person."

He'd feigned a stab to the heart. "Ouch."

"You know what I mean."

He sat on the towel next to her, rested his elbows on his bent knees. "I'd like kids."

"How many?" She sat up.

"Two, I think."

"I want four," she'd replied.

His eyebrows climbed high above his sunglasses. "Four? That's a lot."

She shrugged. "What can I say? I like kids. They're fun, and they don't judge you."

"Four kids, huh? I could live with that."

She'd felt such a warmth drift through her spirit in that moment. As though they were both on the same path. He wanted the same things she did. He saw her as a potential wife, someone to build a family with. It was romantic and touching. She thought she'd found her person at twenty-three years old. It was perfect timing. She was ready to settle down and start a family. And it seemed he was too.

But two years later, nothing much had changed. He'd never spoken of having a family again. Hadn't mentioned picking out a ring or marriage. And every month that passed by, he'd pulled away from her a little at a time, until they barely spoke about anything meaningful. She hadn't noticed at first. Now, looking back, she could see the trajectory of their relationship spiralling, but she couldn't figure out why. She tried ruminating over the various stages of their two years together but drew a blank. All she could think was that maybe he didn't appreciate her. He said he loved her, but did he really?

She'd been so blind.

To so many things.

Who was she? Where was she from ... really? Was she in love? Did she have brothers and sisters? What about her parents?

There were so many questions running about her thoughts like whirligig beetles skating across a river. And she had no answers. Not yet, anyway. That's what the trip would be about. Finding answers. Discovering the truth after all these years. There'd been so many secrets, so much buried. She didn't know who to trust anymore. Everyone had lied to her. Or maybe some of them had lied and others hadn't known they were lying. Was it still lying if you didn't know?

Stella hadn't lied. Her sister was one of the few people she trusted completely. Although she'd seen the look on Stella's face when she finally understood that nothing she'd been told was true. Stella may not have known, but she suspected, at the very least, because it wasn't a shock to her. Not in the way it had been to Matilda. Not in the *my whole world is coming crashing down around me* kind of way that had shaken Matilda to her core. That wasn't the way it happened for Stella, she could tell. Her sister's eyes always gave her away. But she claimed not to know a thing, of course. So did both of their brothers. Innocent, naive, unaware—whichever way she sliced it, they claimed to be in the dark as much as she was. And no one seemed to know what to do next. They didn't support her journey; they all thought she was crazy for trying. That she'd only bring herself heartache. And of course, they were probably right. What did she know?

"Georgia."

She said the word beneath her breath, then quickly looked around to see if anyone heard. No one seated at the gate was paying her any attention. A girl two seats over had headphones in and was slumped down in her chair, eyes shut. There was an elderly couple a few chairs over, trying their best to pull on compression stockings, their bare feet resting on top of their joggers while they argued back and forth about the best way to manage it—roll or fold, pull first or bunch up around the ankle and then pull.

Georgia was a place she'd never once thought about in her entire life. And now it could be the very crux of everything she needed to know about herself. It might hold all the answers. Or it could be a complete dead end.

What did she know about the place? Heat. It was supposed to be hot and humid. And the locals had thick accents. The word *peaches* sprang to mind, followed quickly by football and hot wings. And she was out. She didn't know one more thing about the southern state. She'd looked it up briefly before booking her flight but didn't have time to investigate any more than that. She could do that now, since she was seated at the gate with nothing else going on, but she wasn't sure she wanted to. Her anxiety was playing up, and the last thing she needed was to stoke that particular bear any more than she had to. No, she'd rather show up in Georgia and find her way from there. She'd booked a hotel for the first night. But after that, she'd have to figure it out. And the thought of that made her head spin.

This was a good thing, she reminded herself. She was

twenty-five years old and had never really challenged herself. Had never travelled like most young Australians did. Had never faced down the unknown. And it was time. She didn't want to become a nervous invalid who couldn't manage a plane flight without a panic attack. She was a veterinarian, rock climber, marathon runner, and kayaker. She could handle a little bit of open-ended travel. Surely it couldn't be that hard to navigate her way through an English-speaking country.

But it wasn't the travel that caused the knot in her stomach. Whatever lay in wait for her, however the truth revealed itself, she wasn't sure she could handle it. It might derail her entire sense of self. Her identity was hanging by a thread. She wasn't the type for an existential crisis. But she'd loved her parents with every ounce of her being, and she didn't want that to change now they were gone.

She sighed. Whatever she uncovered when she arrived at her destination would change everything. Was she ready for that?

Chapter Two

TWO MONTHS EARLIER

The charcuterie board balanced on the edge of the table as though threatening to topple over at any moment. Matilda pushed a piece of melba toast covered in camembert and fig jam into her mouth and then used her hip to prod the board back into place. She nodded in satisfaction as she smoothed the lace-trimmed white tablecloth with a tug. The table was laden with good food—roasted chicken, bread rolls, salads, muffins. Anything the dozens of mourners could think to bring was there. A hodgepodge of kindness and sympathy in gastronomical form served to comfort those in attendance.

Matilda glanced around the room as she chewed, noting the clusters of people gathered together in small groups and speaking in hushed tones. There were her father's colleagues by the grand piano, and the church folks next to the large horse-riding landscape in watercolour. Her cousins had congregated by the punch bowl. And her siblings huddled together along the far wall beneath the family portraits.

She grabbed another melba toast, slathered cheese on it,

and hurried to join them. Stella, her sister, sat with hunched shoulders, nursing a glass of white wine in one hand. Her eyes looked glazed with dark smudges staining the skin beneath them. Matilda rested a hand on Stella's back as she sat in the empty chair beside her.

"How are you doing, sis?"

Stella inhaled a quick breath as though waking up. "I'm ok. You?"

"Meh." Matilda ate the snack in her hand as she listened in on her brother's conversation.

"I don't think Dad would've wanted you to get rid of the Porter painting," Bryce stated emphatically. "And besides, he knew I wanted to keep it. It reminds me of him." His voice broke.

"Well, I'm the executor, so it's up to me." Todd crossed his arms. "And there's so much to go through, we can't get emotional about every little thing."

"That doesn't mean you can do whatever you want," Bryce objected.

Matilda forced a wry smile onto her face. "Not today, please. Can we talk about all this tomorrow? Today's not the right time."

Both brothers looked at her. Todd's face softened and he patted her shoulder. "You're right. We'll talk about it later."

Bryce grunted. "Fine, we'll talk about something else." He eyed the table. "I don't think I can eat anything."

"It's all I can do," Matilda replied with a grimace, still licking her lips. "Someone stop me."

She pushed her long, blonde hair back over her shoulder, regretting wearing it down for the hundredth time as sweat trickled down her spine.

"You can get away with it," Stella complained with a gentle shoulder shove. "It goes right to my hips."

"You can't claim that every single thing you eat goes

directly to your hips. Metabolism doesn't work that way," Todd said, with a shake of his head.

"It does with me. My metabolism is different to anyone else's."

"That's scientifically impossible," Bryce chimed in.

"I'm a scientific marvel," Stella replied with a wink at Matilda who couldn't help but laugh.

She wrapped an arm around her sister's shoulders. "You're definitely a marvel."

"But honestly, how is it you managed to get blonde hair, tanned skin, and narrow hips? Plus that tiny waist? It's so unfair. When here I am, big hips, tiny boobs, freckled skin and brown curls."

Matilda's throat tightened. She missed her mother. "You look like Mum." Her eyes filled with tears, but she tried to smile them away. "I love the way you look."

Stella's eyes filled, and she blinked hard. "Don't start. I don't want to cry anymore. My throat hurts, my head's got some kind of mallet whacking against the inside of my skull, and I'm ready to crash on my bed for twelve solid hours."

Matilda reached for her sister's hand and held it tight. "We just have to get through the next hour. Then everyone will leave, and we can go to bed."

"After we clean up," Stella replied.

"I'm hoping someone else will stay to do that."

"Don't hold your breath," Bryce hissed as he nodded a thank you at a well-wisher.

A steady stream of mourners continued by their chairs, giving their sympathies as they came and went. The four siblings had already gotten used to plastering a thin smile on their faces, nodding their heads, and muttering a soft thank you in response. Although Matilda wasn't sure how much more she could manage.

The house was full to the brim of people her parents had

loved and shared their lives with. But so many of them were people she didn't know or had only met once or twice. She'd left home when she was eighteen. That was seven years ago. And her parents had lived full lives in that time between work, the church, the lawn bowls club and their horse-riding group. When her mother died two years earlier, Dad's circle had shrunk a little. But most of her mother's friends had continued to drop by every now and then to check on him. It was a tight-knit community in the beachside town of Kingscliff.

"You know, with Mum and Dad both dying of cancer, I think it's time we talk about getting tested," Todd said, in his best doctor voice.

"I don't know..." Stella said. "Is that really necessary?"

"We should check to see if we have the gene," Todd replied. "It could be lifesaving for all of us."

"I guess we could do that," Bryce added. "Where would we go?"

"I can do it in the lab at the hospital," Todd replied.

"Okay, well, I guess we should line it up while we're all here," Matilda said, glancing at her smart watch to check for messages. She wasn't sure when she'd get a chance to go back to Brisbane, but projects were piling up and she needed to get on top of it. There were rumours of impending layoffs at the graphic design studio where she'd only been working for the past six months, and she didn't want to give them an excuse to add her name to the list. "I might not get back to Kingscliff for a while."

"You're always dying to get out of here," Stella said with a pout. "Can't you stay for a while. We're going to need your help with getting the house sorted."

"I suppose I could do some work in Dad's office. I brought my laptop with me."

"That would be good," Todd said. "We all have work to

do, but we've got to make some decisions and sort through Dad's paperwork. There are so many unknowns at this point."

Matilda knew that Todd liked to have everything organised. His thick brown hair was always perfectly combed to one side. He had the physique of a man who never skipped a gym workout. He hated for anything to be uncertain. And the fact that he wasn't sure yet what their father's will contained, or exactly what he should do with everything in their parents' estate, made him uncomfortable. But it didn't bother Matilda. She took things as they came. There wasn't anything else she could do other than accept life the way it was.

"Speaking of tests," Stella began, "have any of you done that DNA test kit Dad got us all for Christmas yet?"

"The family history one?" Bryce asked. "No, not yet. I can't remember where I put it."

"I haven't looked at it," Matilda admitted. "Besides, I have no idea why Dad gave us a DNA test kit for Christmas. We all know what it's going to say. We're Irish, Scottish and French, don't we already know that?"

Stella shrugged. "You look Swedish to me. So who knows?"

Matilda had heard the same thing all her life. Wherever she went, people asked about her Scandinavian heritage—she had none. Not as far as she knew. They also questioned why she looked so different from the rest of her family. And of course, when she was a kid, there were the inevitable jokes about being the postman's daughter. Her own father had dark hair, hazel eyes, and fair skin, just like the rest of the family. Still, she was used to it. It didn't bother her the way it had when she was younger.

"Okay, enough with the jokes. If you care about it so much, I'm happy to take the test. We can do all our tests at one time and get it over with. Find out if we really do have Swedish heritage and whether we're all likely to die of cancer. Sounds like an absolute riot." She rolled her eyes.

Stella laughed softly. "Don't do it if you don't want to."

"No, no, I'm sure it's going to be fun. I've always wanted to know if I'm destined to die early." She tended to delve into sarcastic retorts when she was feeling emotional but was too tired to cry. She'd cried so much over the past week, she was fairly certain she was seriously dehydrated.

"Fine, it's settled," Bryce said. "We'll do all the tests. And we'll figure out what to do with Dad's things. And, well..." He swallowed, unable to finish his sentence.

But Matilda knew what he was about to say. They would be finished with Kingscliff. All four of them lived in the city. And now that Dad was gone, they'd have no reason to return. It was their childhood home, and she loved the place, but other than the occasional holiday, would she spend time there again? Probably not. She was busy with her life in the city. Her boyfriend was making noise about moving in, although she'd already told him she wasn't that kind of girl. So maybe he would propose. She was well and truly ready. They'd dated for two years. She'd hoped to get married before Mum died, but he hadn't taken the hint.

Surely, it would be soon.

Regardless, the fact was, Kingscliff was her past. Brisbane was her present. She had no idea what her future held, but she hoped it would be a family, a thriving career, and an annual trip back to the seaside town of her childhood to swim in the surf and catch up with family. They'd been through so much grief over the past few years, nursing sick parents and watching them fade away. She was ready for some relief. It was time for her life to begin. To put the past behind her and step into a new adventure.

Chapter Three

The roar of the rubbish truck almost deafened Matilda as she wheeled her bicycle out from the garden shed beside her small townhouse. As it accelerated away, she adjusted her helmet and peered down the street. Traffic was consistent at this time of the morning, with everyone in Brisbane on their way to work. The sun already shone hot overhead, and there was a strong scent of rain on summer grass in the air. It'd poured buckets overnight, and the summer heat was doing its best to grow every lawn in the city faster than anyone could manage to mow it into submission.

A magpie on her quiet Tarragindi street took great pleasure in dive bombing her each morning. However, it wasn't the diving that bothered Matilda, it was the clacking of the bird's beak as it swept past her ear that always made her heart miss a beat. She never quite knew when to expect it, and already, her pulse was accelerating in anticipation of the encounter. She'd taken to riding this stretch of her commute with a large stick held high over her head. It seemed to do the trick. But this morning, she hadn't been able to find it. Her neighbour, Mrs Primrose, had probably thrown it away. She liked the yard to be neat and tidy with nothing out of place.

Just as she was about to climb onto her bike, her mobile phone buzzed in her pants pocket. She set the bike against the fence and pulled out the phone, then walked to the concrete front steps to sit as she answered it.

"Hello?"

"Hey, Tilly." The nickname Stella had given her when they were kids had stuck. The entire family called her Tilly, and even some of her friends.

"How are you? Back into the swing of life?" They'd all left Kingscliff the day before after two weeks together, and it felt strange to return to the usual routine now that Dad was gone. She already missed her siblings and the big old house he'd left behind, which now sat empty.

"It's weird. I wanted to call Dad this morning to tell him about my DNA test results. They were waiting in my inbox when I got home. Then I remembered that I couldn't. Did you read yours yet?"

Matilda frowned as she put the phone on speaker and scrolled through her email. "I don't see the email. Oh, here it is. What does yours say?"

"Nothing unusual. I'm mostly English with a bit of Celtic and some French. Just like we thought. Although I was expecting more; I don't know why."

"I'll open mine now." She clicked on the link and a web page flashed onto the screen displaying the percentages of the various ethnicities and regions that had been found in her DNA. "I'm glad we all passed that cancer test."

"For now," Stella replied.

"Yes, no cancer for now. But at least we don't have to worry about hereditary cancer though, after the genetic testing we did. That was a big relief for me."

"Me too," said Stella. "I didn't want to think about it. But now that we have the results, it's taken a load off my shoulders."

Matilda scanned the website, looking for anything that made sense. She grunted. "Hold on, this says I'm German and Nordic. I don't have any English or Celtic. Nothing from France either."

"Well, that's strange," Stella replied. "How can you have different ancestry to me?"

"I don't know. I'm not really sure how these things work. Can I have inherited different aspects of our genes?"

"I don't think so." Stella hesitated. "You've always looked different to the rest of us, but that shouldn't mean anything. Right?"

"Hold on," Matilda said, noticing something. "There's a section on relationships. Do you see that?"

"Oh yeah, I see it. Mine has links to Bryce and Todd. And some of our cousins. Dad's listed there too. He must've done the test before he gave us all a membership on the website for Christmas. He didn't say anything about it though, that's strange."

Matilda's stomach dropped. "I don't have links to any of you."

"What?!" The concern in Stella's voice was evident now. "That can't be right."

"What is going on?" Matilda's voice dropped to a whisper as a knot formed in her gut.

"Do you have anyone listed in the relationships section?"

"Yes, there's a surname, but no first name. Someone has chosen to be anonymous on here. At least, that's how it looks. The name is Osbourne. And apparently, I'm their cousin, at least I think that's what it shows."

"Osbourne?" Stella asked. "I don't know anyone with that last name. Does it say where they're located?"

"It looks like they're in Georgia, in the southern part of the United States."

"They must've mixed your test up with someone else's," Stella said firmly. "That's all this is. We don't have any relatives in the USA. So, it has to be a mistake."

Matilda pressed her lips together. None of this made any sense. How could she have a link to someone she'd never heard of on the other side of the world? And why did none of her heritage align with her sister's? They'd always joked that she was the postman's daughter, and other lighthearted jabs about her looks, her talents, and everything about her that made her different to the rest of the family. But maybe there was more to it. Could it be true though? Surely her parents would've said something if she were adopted? The idea that she might've been adopted made her throat ache. This couldn't be happening.

"I wish we'd never taken the test," she muttered, suddenly angry. "I told you I didn't want to do it."

"No, you didn't," Stella objected.

"Well, I should've said something because I was against it from the beginning. I knew it would be trouble."

"Tilly ... don't get upset. I'm sure it's a mistake. We'll figure it out."

"That's easy for you to say. You're not the one who's probably adopted and whose parents never told her."

"I'm sure that's not the case."

Matilda could tell that she wasn't sure of any such thing. All the force had drained from her voice, and it sounded weak and strained.

"Why didn't Dad say anything? Instead, he gave us these DNA test kits that we might never have used."

"I don't know," Stella replied with a sigh. "I suppose this was his way of prodding you into investigating it."

"But he could've said something." Matilda was exasperated. Why hadn't her father simply pulled her aside and talked to her about this? What had he been hiding? Or did he think the test kits were a cute gift and knew nothing about what she'd find? They would never have clarity. He was gone. So was her mother.

"We should ask Auntie Flora about it," she said suddenly, her eyes widening. "She's bound to know the truth."

Flora was their mother's older sister and the two of them had been very close. Flora had recently been a little forgetful though, so it would be interesting to see if they could get any useful information out of her.

"Great idea," Stella replied. "I'll call her later, see if she's around tonight. We can go over there, take some cake. She'll be talking in no time. I'm certain of it."

Matilda finished the phone call and climbed onto her bike. She set off pedalling down the road, lost in thought. This was clearly some kind of misunderstanding. It couldn't be true. The lab had messed up. They'd switched her test results with someone else's. It was the only plausible explanation. But in the back of her mind, the same niggling doubts that'd plagued her childhood bothered her brain.

She'd always wondered why she was so different from everyone else in her family. Even studying biology had confused her—why did both parents have brown eyes and she had blue? It didn't make sense. At the time, when she'd questioned her science teacher, they'd made some kind of remark about one parent having hazel eyes. Which made sense. Dad's eyes had been more hazel than a true brown. Still, every other kid in the family, every cousin, uncle, aunt and grandparent, had brown or hazel eyes. And yet hers were a piercing light blue. They stood out. They made her different in a way that was hard to ignore. And now, she finally had no choice—the truth was tapping at the doorway of her soul, and she couldn't look away any longer.

* * *

Auntie Flora's house was a hour away from where Matilda lived. Her sprawling bungalow was set in five acres of bushland in the Sunshine Coast hinterland. It was beautiful and wild with dense green trees and long, thick grass. It could definitely do with a bit of elbow grease, since the house was in desperate need of a new coat of paint and the mailbox hung askew, but Matilda loved it there. She had so many good childhood memories of visiting the "farm" as they'd called it. Although there weren't any farm animals these days.

They found Flora in the back garden with a watering can in hand and an oversized straw hat on top of her grey hair. Sweat beaded on her upper lip which Matilda noticed was stretched into a smile.

"Well, I wasn't expecting you two," Flora said, as she embraced them one at a time.

"I called earlier," Stella said. "You told me you'd be home."

"It's still so hot out," Flora replied, deftly ignoring Stella's words. "Let's go inside. I've got the air-conditioning running, and I'll put on a pot of tea."

They went inside and sat in the sunny breakfast room at the back of the house overlooking the extensive gardens. They were a little overgrown these days, but it seemed Flora still spent most of her time there. Matilda had fond memories of picking sugar peas and eating them by the handful on hot summer mornings around Christmas time when they would often visit for a week or two. And some of Matilda's favourite childhood memories happened there.

Flora fussed around the kitchen, boiling the kettle to make tea. She set some scones on a plate with small bowls of homemade blueberry jam and freshly whipped cream. Then, they all sat together on the lumpy, old wicker furniture that had seen better days.

"This is lovely, but you didn't have to go to so much trouble," Stella said.

"No trouble at all. I don't get to see my favourite nieces often enough. I wish you'd called, I would've changed clothes."

"We did call," Matilda began, then changed tact. "We had some questions to ask, Auntie Flora. About Mum and Dad."

"And about Matilda," Stella continued, making eye contact with her sister.

Matilda's heart was in her throat. What would Flora say? Would the next few minutes change everything? She wasn't sure what she wanted to hear—that the DNA test was a mistake, or that she'd been adopted and everyone had hidden it from her. Even allowing the thought to flit across her conscious mind felt wrong, like a betrayal of her loving parents.

Flora raised a cup to her lips and sipped the hot tea. Then set it down again. "What is it, my darlings?"

Stella cleared her throat. "Dad gave us all DNA testing kits for Christmas."

Flora arched a thin, grey eyebrow. "He did? Why?"

"We're not exactly sure." Matilda replied. "But maybe there was something he wanted us to know, that he hadn't gotten around to telling us."

Flora shrugged. "I doubt that. He was always an open book."

"But when I did the test, it returned a really strange result, and I'm trying to understand it."

"What do you mean?" Flora asked, her brown eyes finding Matilda's blue ones.

"There doesn't seem to be any connection between my DNA and my siblings. They're all connected to one another, but I'm not."

Flora's eyes clouded, as though she had been transported

far away. She gazed out the window. "Hmm ... must be an error."

"Do you think so? There's nothing else to it?" Stella asked, worry etched in a line between her eyebrows.

"It doesn't make any sense." Flora shook her head slowly. "I was there. I saw you born. Your mother wanted me to be in the room. We were close, you see. Our whole lives, as close as two sisters can be. Your father didn't want to be in the room. Not many fathers did in those days. But I was there. And you came out healthy and huge with a red face and ready to bawl. You've always been a strong one, my dear."

Stella sighed and slapped her thighs with both hands. "Well, there you have it. I knew it was a mistake." She smiled. "Phew! I'm glad we can put that behind us. There's no arguing with Auntie Flora's personal witness, Tilly. Let's eat our scones and forget all about it."

Chapter Four

Four weeks later, Matilda had almost forgotten about the DNA test when Stella asked her to meet up for dinner. Their brothers were coming too, which was the closest thing to a miracle she'd experienced in years. They were both married and always busy with their own families, and they rarely had time for their sisters. If she was being honest, they'd barely spent any time with their parents before they passed either. But she was trying to be more generous of spirit lately. It made her less anxious. She'd been listening to a podcast that outlined strategies for reducing anxiety over the previous few weeks—one such strategy was to give up expectations around the behaviour of others. It'd been helping, even if she found it hard to do at times.

Grief had done some strange things to her in both her mind and body. She'd expected to feel sad, but there was more to it. An emptiness, lack of purpose or direction she hadn't felt before, along with an array of physical symptoms—the worst being her anxiety. It was as though she was existing solely on the shots of adrenaline coursing through her veins somedays. And she was so very tired of it.

It didn't help that work had been manic lately.

"Dr. Berry?" The veterinarian assistant cocked her head to one side. "Did you hear me?"

Matilda focused, glancing up from the paperwork in front of her to give her full attention. "Sorry, Sue. What did you say?"

"Do you want me to keep the chocolate eating labradoodle overnight for observation, or can she go home?"

Matilda smiled. "She can go. I'll come and speak to the owner in a moment."

With a nod, Sue pushed back through the doorway to the reception area and was gone. Matilda continued smiling as she finished filling out the timesheet for the previous patient, a cockatoo with a malting problem, and thought about the labradoodle. She was a beautiful little thing, reddish brown with floppy ears and a mop of curly wool. She'd torn apart a box of chocolates meant as a gift, consuming the lot in twenty minutes while her owner was at the shops. But some charcoal and fluids had done the trick, and she was ready to go home and get some rest. Many dogs fretted if they stayed too long, so she preferred to let them recuperate in a familiar environment if possible.

After she'd dealt with the labradoodle, she returned to her office with a sigh. She was done for the day, and her entire body ached with relief. She'd spent most of the past ten hours on her feet. There'd been two emergency surgeries, plus the chocolate-filled and very hyper dog. Along with five different creatures to euthanise. And a litter of puppies to vaccinate. Along with the usual walk-ins. It'd been a busy day. Something that'd been happening a lot more in recent months, since their veterinary clinic was growing in popularity.

She'd wanted this for a long time but now the achievement felt empty. She didn't even know who she was.

The thought came out of nowhere. Why had those words

run through her mind? She'd put the whole DNA test behind her. Forgotten about it. It was a mistake, nothing more. Auntie Flora had said so—she was there when Matilda was born. A living witness to the event. There was no other explanation other than administrative error. And she'd gone on with her life for four whole weeks, pushing the mistake out of her mind. But now it was back, out of nowhere.

Her phone rang. It was Cam, her boyfriend of two years. She hadn't seen him all week. He'd been less attentive lately. She wondered if there was something wrong.

She answered with what she hoped sounded like enthusiasm. "Hey, Cam."

"Hi, honey. Sorry I haven't called lately. It's been busy at work, and I'm training for that half marathon..."

She interrupted him. "It's fine, don't worry about it. How are you?"

"I'm good. My calf muscles are really tight ... anyway, that's not important. I thought we could get some dinner?"

"I'm sorry, I've already committed to dinner with my brothers and Stella, which is a pretty rare occurrence. So I don't think I can blow them off this late in the day."

"No, of course you can't. We can have drinks afterwards. Does that work for you?"

"Sounds good. I'm hopeless at staying up late, but I'll make it work, since I'm dying to see you." She hadn't missed him as much as she should've, but the past couple of months had taken a toll on her. Maybe her emotions were used up and she didn't have enough left over for him.

* * *

"Let's drink shots!" Bryce said, eyes gleaming with mischief as he raised a hand to signal the waiter.

The restaurant he'd chosen was loud and packed full of

diners. It was a far trendier nightspot than Matilda had visited in years. These days, she preferred to sit on her couch with a cat on either side, eating takeaway, than to go to a nightclub or a popular bar in the city. But Bryce had booked it for them to eat dinner together, and so far, she was enjoying herself. Until he'd said the word "shots", anyway.

"Shots? I don't know..." Matilda began.

Stella laughed. "Really, Bryce? We're not teenagers anymore."

"I never drank shots when I was a teen..." Todd said with a flare of his nostrils.

Did Todd ever let his hair down? Matilda couldn't remember the last time he'd relaxed. He was a busy doctor, popular in his field. He had to be responsible, she understood that. But they were family, and he'd caught an Uber to the restaurant, there was no reason for him to be a stick in the mud. Pulling her hairband out of her hair in a symbolic gesture, she shook it free, letting the golden waves fall about her shoulders.

"Okay, Bryce, let's do shots."

It didn't take much convincing to get Stella and Todd on board. And while they waited for the modern Asian fusion food to arrive, they drank shots of Tequila until Matilda's head began to feel light and her words slurred.

Todd's voice immediately grew louder as he shouted over the noise of the crowd. "If my hands are injured tonight, I hold you all personally responsible."

Matilda rolled her eyes. "No one is going to injure your precious hands, sweetie. Relax. I love it when you let go of that stick..." she bit down on her tongue.

"What stick?" Bryce asked, eyes narrowing.

Stella burst out laughing then clamped a hand over her mouth. Eyes wide, she said. "I—ve definitely shoulda n—ot had that last one."

Bryce giggled silently beside her, his whole body shaking. "You guys, I love you. You're the best."

"I love you too," Matilda replied. "All of you. I'm so grateful for you. But I miss you. We don't do this often enough."

"Now that Mum and Dad are gone, we've got to make the effort," Bryce said.

"Definitely," Stella agreed, nodding emphatically.

Their food arrived and they made space for it on the table, moving the empty shot glasses out of the way. Bryce ordered a bottle of red wine for them to share, and Matilda poured it for them. Then, she spooned food from each of the shared plates onto her own. It was hot, spicy, and looked delicious. Thinly sliced beef, fat, juicy prawns, fried balls of breaded chicken and pork, all made with vegetables, onions and peppers into meals that mixed Australian and Asian cultures together.

She took a bite of the beef and savoured the tangy flavour. "Mmmm ... this is good."

"You're right, Bryce," Todd said, picking up the threads of their conversation. "Now that our parents are no longer here, we won't be meeting up at their house for the holidays. We can't just bump into each other over a family lunch. We're going to have to be the ones who stay in touch." His brow was furrowed. "I guess I hadn't thought much about it."

"It's been easy to let our connection slip a bit over the years," Stella said. "But I'll try to call more often."

They all agreed to do the same.

"We're all we have," Matilda said, thoughtfully. Although, the idea brought tears to her eyes.

"You've got Cam too," Stella replied, lovingly patting her arm.

Matilda sniffled into a napkin. "I know, but it's not the same. I'm not even sure things will work out there."

"What? Why not?" Stella asked, alarm written on her face. "You two have been together for ages."

"He's not right for you," Todd added, before taking a big bite of pork.

Matilda glared at him. "What do you mean by that?"

"You know what I mean. He's a bit ... I don't know. Self-absorbed."

She wanted to point out the irony of Todd making such a statement. But the steam quickly abated when she realised he was right. She couldn't refute his argument. And even though Todd could be annoying, he was most often right, which was actually one of his more annoying traits.

"You can definitely do better," Bryce added with a nod. A brown curl fell over his eyes, and he blew it back with a huff of air.

"Which leaves me exactly where I said ... alone, apart from you guys. You're all I have. And what if...?" She choked back a sob. When she drank, she always got emotional and talkative. She couldn't help it. All the things she'd been burying came rushing to the surface, with nothing holding them back any longer.

"What's wrong, honey?" Stella asked, with concern etched on her pretty face.

"What if I'm not actually your sister?"

"What are you talking about?" Todd asked as he paused eating, fork halfway to his mouth.

Bryce frowned at her. "Tilly, what's going on?"

Matilda exchanged a look with Stella, who offered her a wan smile. She drew a deep breath, willing her spinning mind to focus. "I didn't tell you two about it, but when my DNA results came back from that test we took, it showed that I wasn't related to any of you."

Bryce screwed up his nose. "No, that's silly. It can't be right."

"I'm sure there's a reasonable explanation. Don't go getting upset about," Todd added with a nod.

"We went to see Auntie Flora," Stella said. "And she told us she saw Tilly born. So, I agree—it's got to be a mistake. You shouldn't worry about it, Tilly."

"Why aren't any of you telling me to call the company? Complain? Get to the bottom of it?" Matilda asked, feeling a lump grow in her throat.

Stella sighed and looked at Todd, who promptly flicked his gaze towards his brother. There was silence.

"It's nothing, really," Stella said suddenly with a bright smile. "Only ... I don't really want to know. That's all."

"Me either," Bryce added, reaching over to squeeze Matilda's hand. "It doesn't matter either way. Don't dig into it. We're fine. We're a team. I'm certain it's an error, but if it's not... — well, I don't think it'll benefit us to find out."

"You've got to know." Todd said, with consternation. "You can't just hide from the truth."

Matilda looked back and forth between them. Her siblings all had their eyes fixed on her face with worried expressions. She loved her family so much. "Todd's right, I want to know the truth. I wasn't going to pursue it. I tried to get on with my life. But I've got to find out if there's something real behind these results."

"Oh honey..." Stella said.

"It's going to be okay," Todd added. "No matter what, it doesn't change anything."

"We're your family," Bryce said.

She nodded, the lump in her throat almost choking her now. "I know. But thanks for saying it."

Chapter Five

By the time she'd finished dinner with her brothers and sister, Matilda had sobered up a little bit. But she still felt like dropping directly into bed and yawned as she climbed out of the taxi to walk into the bar where she was meeting Cam. It wasn't as crowded as the restaurant had been, with only a few people grouped in clusters around the darkened space.

Cam waited in a booth at the far end of the room and waved when she approached. He stood to kiss her, then she sat across from him. The brown faux leather seats squeaked as she shifted position.

"What would you like to drink?" he asked.

She glanced at the bar. "A Tom Collins please."

"I'll be right back."

He soon returned with their drinks. A beer for him and a lemon flavoured cocktail for her. He wore his light brown hair long, with it pulled back into a messy bun at the nape of his neck. His glasses were black-rimmed and his style was in line with most of the young men of his age in the city—skinny jeans with a black t-shirt.

They'd dated for two years, but it felt shorter than that.

Had they ever been serious? She'd thought they were, but after so much time together, he still hadn't spoken about the future or plans for moving their relationship to the next level in a long time. And she'd hadn't brought it up either. Perhaps because she didn't want to. If she was honest with herself, she couldn't imagine marrying him. But dating was comfortable. She enjoyed his company, they were a good match on paper. It would be a mistake to end things simply because she wasn't head over heels. Wouldn't it?

She sipped her drink and smiled at him. "How was work?"

He shrugged. "This project is going to be the death of us. The whole team is exhausted. I feel like I haven't seen you much in weeks. The deadline is Tuesday, so we'll probably be working all weekend. Sorry, that reminds me, I'm going to have to cancel our beach outing on Saturday."

"That's fine," she said. "I understand. Hopefully you get this finished and can take a break."

He nodded. "That's the plan."

"Remember me telling you about that DNA test I did?"

He gulped a mouthful of beer before replying. "Uh huh."

"I think I'm going to pursue it. Find out what happened there. I need to know the truth."

"That could be dangerous. You might find something you don't want to know."

Why was everyone so against her looking into the results? "You don't think I can handle it?"

He sighed. "That's not what I'm saying. Although, if it does turn out that you're not related to your family, that could cause some real angst."

"I know that." She stared at her Tom Collins. "But I've got to do it anyway. Now that it's out there, I won't ever be able to put it behind me until I figure it out."

He leaned back against the upholstery. "Why don't you

upload your DNA to one of those sites that tells you who your family are?"

"Do you think that's the best approach?"

"Why not? If you really want the truth, that's probably the fast-track method to get there."

Nerves jangled in her gut. If she did this, there'd be no turning back. She hated the idea of not being related to her siblings, aunts, uncles, cousins. They were her family, all she had. And that link felt more and more tenuous the longer she considered the possibility that it was false.

"Okay, I suppose that would be a good place to start."

He smiled. "Now, let's talk about Sunday. We were meant to go to that Jazz festival with Gemma and Bart, but..."

"You're working?" she interjected.

He nodded.

* * *

A week later, Matilda was in the middle of treating a client when the text message came in. She heard her phone buzz but couldn't get to it in that moment. A long-time patient, a golden-haired cocker spaniel, was there to be euthanised, and her owner was sobbing silently.

"I'll leave you alone for a few minutes and then we'll be underway," Matilda said quietly, one hand on the client's arm.

The client nodded, sniffled into a handkerchief. Matilda quietly slipped out the door, then retrieved her phone from the pocket of her long, white coat. The message was from the genetic tracing website she'd submitted her DNA to after her conversation with Cam.

Her heart skipped a beat. When she opened this message, it might turn her world upside down. Was she ready for that?

She hurried to her office and shut the door, then sat in the closest chair.

The message was brief, giving her a link to click for a full report. When she opened it, she wasn't sure what she was looking at for a minute. Then, it all became clear.

The report showed only one close relative connection, and that relative was in the United States, in a place called Covington, Georgia. And the connection was a cousin.

How? What? She shook her head, narrowed her eyes at the screen. That couldn't be right. She had a cousin in Georgia? She'd read the fine print. Unless a person was also listed on this website with their DNA profile, the connection wouldn't show up. Her brothers and sister in Australia had never submitted their results to this website, so she wasn't expecting them to be linked to her. But her initial DNA report had already ruled that out, if it was correct.

The possibility of a cousin on the other side of the world made her head spin. She couldn't wrap her mind around how that was possible. Her uncle had spent some time in the USA when he was in the military. Perhaps something had happened then, and he hadn't mentioned it to his family out of embarrassment. Or maybe he didn't know.

Did this mean her uncle had an affair?

She had to pay a fee to see the name of the cousin on the website. She did that, and then studied the name for a moment.

Tyler Osbourne.

There it was again, the name Osbourne. The same name that'd been listed in the DNA report. She said his name out loud, then shoved her phone in her pocket. On her way back to the examination room, she made a decision. She wanted to talk to Tyler, find out about him. He was her cousin, according to the DNA results. And it was time she learned the truth. It seemed she'd been lied to for the past twenty-five years. And she didn't want to go one more birthday without knowing her birth family.

* * *

At home later that night, she stared at the family connection report on her laptop. With a half-drunk glass of red wine in hand, she typed his name into the search bar.

There were far too many results. So she added *Covington Georgia*. And a cafe was the first result. The Honeysuckle Cafe. It sounded nice. She wasn't sure why the search engine had chosen the cafe for her results, it didn't include Tyler's name anywhere on the website. She scrolled through it, looking for clues. Then, on the *About* page, she saw another Osbourne.

The cafe's owner shared a last name with Tyler—Rita Osbourne. And the cafe was located in Covington. That couldn't be a coincidence. Or maybe it was, and the search algorithm didn't know what it was talking about. But still, whoever this Rita person was, she might know Tyler. Unless Covington was a big place, she had no idea. She wasn't even quite sure where Georgia was located on the map.

She pulled up a map then located Georgia right above Florida in the south-eastern corner of the United States of America. She didn't know much about that part of the world. Wasn't *Gone with the Wind* set it Georgia? She'd loved that book when she was eighteen. She'd had a stage of reading as many historical classics as she could get her hands on when she was about fourteen. And that particular book had stood out to her as something special.

The cafe website had a phone number listed at the bottom of the *About* page. On a whim, she picked up her phone and dialled. The number didn't work. Since it was an international call, she likely had to use some kind of country code. She looked it up, and then added the prefix. This time the phone rang.

It rang ten times, and she was about to hang up when someone answered. The woman sounded sleepy.

"Hello, Honeysuckle Cafe, this is Rita."

Matilda hesitated. She wasn't sure what to say now that she had the person on the phone. "Oh, uh, hi. My name is Matilda..."

"Huh? honey, you're gonna have to speak up. I can't hear you."

She cleared her throat and raised her voice. "I'm Matilda, from Australia. And I was calling to ask if you know a man called Tyler Osbourne."

"There's something wrong with this dang phone. I can't hear much but gobbly-de-gook. And if you're selling somethin', I'm not buying. Have a great day, honey."

The phone line disconnected, and Matilda stared at the wall for a few long moments. This was ridiculous. She couldn't call a cafe on the other side of the world and ask the woman who owned it whether she knew her biological cousin. The United States was a big place, and Osbourne was a common surname. What she really should do is travel there, visit the cafe as a starting point, and see where the breadcrumbs led. If they led anywhere at all. Surely, if she had her feet on the ground there, she would be able to track down her cousin.

Chapter Six

Rita Osbourne hung up the phone with a frown. It was getting so bad these days, she might have to change her number. She couldn't understand, for the life of her, those telemarketer phone calls where the caller paused before speaking and then used some kind of heavy accent. They always wanted her to buy something, or switch service providers, or donate money. And she didn't have time for that when she was at work. There was something going on with the refrigerator, everything was melting. She still didn't have enough crab legs for this evening's dinner service. And there was a muddy stink permeating the outside deck, which would make customers none too happy when they came in for lunch.

She shook her head and hurried outside to think about what she could do to camouflage the odour. The fact was, they'd had so much rain lately that everything stunk in that heady kind of way that it always did after heavy rain. It didn't much bother her, but customers were finicky, and she hated to hear them whine. Maybe she could burn some incense, see if that helped. She had some lavender somewhere.

After she located the diffuser and got the lavender oil

burning on the patio, she sat in her small, cramped office behind the pantry to see if she could figure out the crab legs situation. After a few phone calls, it looked as though dinner was saved. She called a refrigerator tradesman, and he promised to visit the cafe later that afternoon. Then, when the manager, Amanda, arrived to start on the lunch service, she packed up her things to head home.

Rita had trained Amanda herself and had handed off the day shift to her at least five years ago. They were a good team. And Rita didn't have the energy she used to when she was in her forties. These days, she was exhausted by the end of the evening and found it hard to get going again the next morning if she'd been on her feet too long. She found that spending the afternoon at home gave her enough rest before she tackled dinner at the cafe.

Amanda poked her head through the office door with the ever-present scowl that Rita had grown accustomed to. "Those crab legs come in?"

"Cal is dropping them over in the next half an hour. Let me know if he's runnin' late. Y'all need to keep an eye on that fridge though. It's acting up again. The fridge man is coming this afternoon, and I hope to goodness he gets it dealt with 'cause I don't have the patience to deal with it today, what with everything else I've got going on."

"You feeling okay, hon?" Amanda asked. "You're looking a touch pale."

"Just tired. I'm gonna get me some rest."

"You do that. I've got this under control."

The drive to the lake house was a short one. The Jackson Lake property had been in her family for generations. And so had the Honeysuckle Cafe. They were thirty minutes apart, and it was a pleasant commute, with large green fields on both sides of the road. Both the lake house and business were left to her by her parents ten years earlier when they'd passed in close succession. And she'd done everything she could to hold onto them, tooth and nail, through two economic downturns, a pandemic, and a lawsuit filed by an entitled customer who had been determined to rip her off. She and her business had made it, just. Although the buildings themselves were a little worse for wear. Both could do with a new coat of paint and a few upgrades. But money was tight, so it would just have to wait.

She glanced in the rearview mirror and sighed—she needed a bit of work done too. She fluffed the wavy, greying hair that fell over her forehead. And did her best to smooth out the wrinkles that fanned out from the corners of her eyes. Of course, they returned the very moment she let go of the loose skin. Sometimes she almost didn't recognise herself. She tried not to look too intently into mirrors these days. An unexpected glimpse of her reflection in a store window often gave her a fright.

Her black Chevy pickup was big and blew smoke when it was feeling ornery. But it did the trick and got her home. That was good enough for now.

Blue, her black lab, barked loudly when she pulled into the driveway. He kept watch over the house while she was gone. She shut the gates to keep him in, although that never seemed to work when he had a mind to wander. These days, though, he stayed put most of the time. He was slowing down just as she was. And she hated to think what she'd do when he was gone.

She climbed out of the truck with a smile and rubbed his head and ears. His tail whacked rhythmically against the truck door. His breath stunk of something disgusting. She didn't want to know what.

"You keep that dang tongue to yourself, boy. Whatever you've been into, I don't want that on my leg. Now stop it!"

The dog looked chagrined, almost mournful, and she

shook her head. "Don't use those puppy dog eyes on me. You know you're not supposed to lick me."

"Hey, Rita!" A man's voice caught her attention, and she spun about to look over the truck's hood.

"Well, what are you doin' home at this time of day, Ryan Merritt?"

Ryan strode over to her, wearing a torn pair of shorts and a grease-stained t-shirt that showed off his strong, tanned arms. His dirty blonde hair spiked out beneath a hat, and his dark sunglasses hid the green eyes that generally sparkled with mischief when he spoke to her.

"I took the day off to get some things done around here. Anything need fixing at yours?"

"Anything...?" She laughed. "A better question would be, is there anything that doesn't need fixing?"

He crossed his arms over his thick chest. "I can look around if you like. See if there's anything urgent."

"I'd appreciate it," Rita replied. "I can't get my head on straight right now. I'm sure it'll come to me right about midnight. But I know there's a broken faucet in the kitchen. Otherwise, I'll have to find that list I was making. It's got to be around here somewhere."

"What have you got planned for the afternoon?"

"I was thinking about taking a big ole nap."

He grinned. "Sounds perfect. I'll make sure to keep it down."

"Have you asked out that woman in the bait shop yet?"

He shrugged. "She's not my type. I told you that."

"I'm dying to know who is your type," Rita said.

"I'll never tell. You'll try to set me up."

She wrinkled her nose. "It's my duty, as an old southern woman, to meddle in your affairs. And you're ruining all my fun. How about Amanda, the manager at the cafe?"

He forced a smile onto his face. "Stop trying to set me up.

I'm a grumpy thirty-five year old man who just wants to be left alone. I don't want a girlfriend, or a wife, or anyone to bother me. Let me fix things around your house in peace, and we'll all be happy."

"Why are you so grouchy? I'm going to start calling you Oscar," she said with a frown.

"I've been there, done that and don't want the t-shirt," he called over his shoulder as he walked away.

"You need love!" she demanded in a loud voice at his retreating back.

With a stamp of her foot, she pondered how frustrating he could be at times. She could help him find happiness, if only he'd let her. She'd always been a good matchmaker. Everyone knew it. Now Ryan simply needed to give in and let her go to work. He'd be forever grateful. She was sure of it.

Even though he could sometimes be the difficult, sullen type, it was nice to have good neighbours. She might live alone, but she never *felt* lonely. There were too many people checking on her at home, at work, and everywhere in between. Ryan had moved in three years earlier when he bought the two-story place next door. It'd needed an entire renovation, which he'd started soon after. He wasn't finished yet, but when he was done, the structure would look incredible. She felt almost ashamed of her single-story, dark, peeling bungalow beside it. Although she couldn't quite embrace the feeling, given how much she loved the place. It was nostalgic, held so many memories of her childhood. She couldn't imagine moving anywhere else.

She unlocked the house and glanced at the unopened stack of mail on the hall table. She'd deal with that later. It would only be bills and such, and she didn't have the energy to face it. Maybe later, after a glass of chilled wine on the deck.

The phone rang, and she shuffled into the kitchen to answer it. Her hip was acting up, and the sciatic pain radiated down her whole right leg, making her knee ache. With a grimace she reached for the phone and answered it.

"Hey Aunt Rita, it's Julie. I can't believe you still have a home phone. You must be the only person in the country who still has a telephone hanging on her kitchen wall."

Rita laughed. "You know I don't get good cell service out here. What if there's an emergency? I've gotta have my phone. Where are you?" Rita's gaze landed on a frame that hung on the wall beside the phone. It held a photograph of her with her sister from ten years earlier. She looked younger, and her sister was gone now. They both had light brown hair with blondish highlights. Now her hair was a dusty blonde and full of grey.

"I'm still in Athens. I've decided not to come home this weekend, so I won't get to see you."

"Oh, that's a shame." Rita loved when Julie visited. Her twenty-five year old niece brought the place to life in a way no one else quite could.

"I'll be back before you know it. I've got too much study to get through. That, plus I got a new job waiting tables at the Magic Mushroom pizzeria. So, I can't miss my shift on Saturday."

"Good for you. That should help with all those little expenses."

"I'm burning through money like I'm on fire." She laughed, a happy tinkling sound that made Rita smile.

"You're doing it right, then." She chuckled. "That's just the way an entitled little sorority girl is supposed to act, isn't it?"

"You know it," Julie quipped.

It was their ongoing joke—Julie had worked hard to pay her way through college. She'd earned a scholarship for the tuition. But she was responsible for her living expenses. Rita helped out when she could, but Julie was proud and liked to do it alone, and so far, she was managing it all pretty well.

She'd clawed her way through undergrad and was now working on a doctorate in psychology.

"How's the cafe?"

"It's still chugging along. We miss you waiting tables. You made the customers happy, that's the truth."

"I miss the tips," Julie groaned. "Never mind, college students tip. Not as well as the folks at your cafe do, but they do okay."

"At least you have all those years of experience to fall back on," Rita said.

"It helps on my resume, for sure."

"And have you decided on a subject for your thesis yet?"

Julie hesitated. "No, not really. It's a lot harder to come up with something unique that contributes to academia than I thought it'd be. Have you been taking those vitamins I bought you?"

"Huh? Which vitamins?"

"I got you some capsules. You said you weren't feeling very energetic. They should help. I hope you haven't lost them already." She could almost hear the eye roll in her niece's voice.

"I'm sure I've just misplaced them. You know how I am. Put them away somewhere for safekeeping. Only the Lord knows where that might be." She chuckled to herself as she padded towards the bedroom. "Listen, honey, I'm going to have a lay down. I'm turning the phone off so it doesn't wake me.

"Okay, I'll see you later but call if you need anything."

Chapter Seven

Cam's black hair stood in stark contrast to the rock wall he clung to. Matilda stared up at him, holding the rope firmly between her hands. She checked her harness again, to make sure it was all connected and attached in the right places. Then, satisfied, returned her attention to her boyfriend's ascent.

"You okay?" She called up at him.

He held out a thumb. "I'm going to come down now. It all looks good."

"Thanks for that."

She released the tension on the rope, and he swung to the ground beside her.

"You sure you want to be the one to climb up?" he asked.

"I'm the vet. I've got to assess the lorikeet when I get to the top, see what's going on before I can decide on an approach."

He shrugged. "It's your call. I'm happy to climb, if you don't want to. I can bring the bird down with me."

"No, I'm good. Thanks, though."

"The rock face is solid. It didn't feel loose. I think you'll be able to make it up to the place where I fixed the rope. And then, you should be able to reach the bird from there."

"Thanks for your help. I couldn't do this without you."

She fixed the rope to her harness and covered her hands in chalk dust. Then stared up at the rocky ledge above her head. She raised her hands and leveraged herself up.

"That wasn't so hard," she muttered to herself. Only about ten metres left to go. She enjoyed rock climbing, but didn't often make it out of the gym. Unlike Cam, who was always off on some wild climbing expedition with his mates. The thought of plummeting to her death was somewhat less appealing to her than it seemed to be to him.

"Did you see the lorikeet?" she called down to him.

He grunted. "I saw grey feathers. I don't know if it's alive, honestly. It wasn't moving."

A climber had called it in. And since she wasn't far away, she'd said she would check it out. It was unusual for her to make off-site appointments like this, but she'd been rostered on for her monthly overnight for taking emergency calls, and she thought it might be a good opportunity to spend time with Cam. If she managed to rescue a bird as well, then that would be a bonus. Although it wasn't sounding hopeful if there was no movement.

She reached the bird within ten minutes. The wall wasn't difficult to climb, and she made her way up with ease. The lorikeet was alive but lethargic. She lifted it into her hands and then positioned it in a bag on her back before abseiling gently down the cliff face.

"I got him," she said, puffing slightly.

He nodded. "Great. I'll pack up."

"Thanks, I've got to work on him."

She took the bird to the vehicle and settled it on a towel before examining it. It seemed to have a broken wing and was probably dehydrated. But other than that, she couldn't tell if there was anything else wrong. She gave it some water with an eye dropper, then wrapped it in the towel and nestled it into a box for the ride back to the clinic.

Cam drove while she held the box containing the bird. He looked over at her. "All okay?"

"He's fine. Probably in shock though. I'm going to be honest, it's hard for birds to come back from that. But we'll do our best."

"Should we grab some dinner after this?"

She nodded. "That would be nice, but I've got to do a few things first."

"Like what?"

"I'm taking a trip to the U.S.A."

"Really? What for?"

She inhaled a quick breath. It would sound ridiculous when she spoke it out loud. She knew that. But this was something she had to do. "I'm going to see if I can find my family."

"Your family is here." He frowned.

"My biological family. You know what I mean. I want to meet them, get to know them, discover where I'm from."

"And that's in America?"

"I'm not really sure. I think I have a relative there. And I'm going to see if I can track him down. Maybe he'll know something and can help me. Maybe he won't. But I've got to try."

He gripped the steering wheel tighter. "I can come with you..."

"I've got to do this on my own. Sorry."

His eyes narrowed. "How long will you be gone?"

"I don't know." She shrugged. "I've already filed the paperwork to take three months of leave from work. I've got long service time accumulated. So, they're fine with it."

"Three months?" he exclaimed. "You can't be serious. You don't want me to come with you, but you'll be gone for months? How does that work?"

She chewed her lower lip, measuring her thoughts. Clearly he was upset, but she wasn't sure exactly which part of her revelation bothered him the most. Lately, his temper had begun to flare up during seemingly random conversations. Was something going on with him she didn't know about?

"I'll call you and keep you updated," she offered.

He shook his head and huffed. "Great, that's just great. My girlfriend will be on the other side of the world for months, but I'll get an occasional phone call. That's not going to work for me, Matilda."

He rarely called her by her first name. Usually it was Honey, or Tilly, or some other cutesy endearment.

"Are you upset about it being so long? Or the fact that I want to go alone?"

He glanced at her, anger narrowing his eyes. "You really don't know?"

"No, I wouldn't ask if I did."

"I don't want to be without a girlfriend for that long. When I started dating you, you had long blonde hair down to your waist, now you've cut it shorter. You used to wear mini-skirts and heels, now all you seem to wear are pants and leggings. You hardly ever want to go drinking with my friends anymore. And now you're going to abandon me for three months. What am I supposed to tell my mates?"

She grimaced. That's what he was upset about? That she no longer fit his image of who she should be, and that his mates might take issue with her absence? Who was this man? It was like she no longer knew him. They'd begun dating when she was twenty-three, only one year out of university. She was young, into the night scene, and enjoyed spending time with the party crowd. But she'd matured since then, mellowed and discovered her inner homebody.

"I had no idea you felt that way about me," she said, sullenly.

"You've changed. I'm not sure we're a good fit any longer. I want someone who looks good on my arm. It matters to my career, and you don't understand how much. You're still beautiful, but you don't make an effort."

Her breath caught in her throat. Did he really just say that?

"And besides, when I'm out with you ... it's bad for my reputation. People notice, they say things. They ask me why I'm dating someone like you when ... well, when I look like me." He pulled the car into the parking lot at the clinic and switched it off with a sigh. "I'm sorry, I know how that sounds. But it's what I feel. People are always telling me to open up, say what I think. So this is me being vulnerable. I've kept it to myself for too long, it's been eating me up."

"Apparently," she replied, pressing a hand to her forehead in disbelief. "So, are you saying you want to break up?"

He faced her, his countenance softening and took one of her hands in his. "You know I care about you, but we're very different people. Let's take this three months as a chance to get some space and think about what we want from life and from each other."

* * *

Matilda sat on the bar stool at her sister's kitchen counter, slumped forward, with her head in her hands. "I can't believe he broke up with me."

"I can't believe he said those things. What a tool!" Stella declared. "You should've dumped him, not the other way around."

"I should've ended things long ago," Matilda agreed. "I've been hanging on because I thought he was better than he seemed. Apparently, I was very wrong about that."

"So, you're really going to America?" Stella asked, as she

stirred slices of chicken into a wok. The chicken sizzled in the oil and steam rose into the air.

It smelled divine and Matilda's stomach growled with hunger.

"I'm going. I've made the decision. I booked a flight last night. It's all happening." Matilda's hunger pangs turned to anxiety and her gut twisted into a knot. "I've never done a long flight like that before."

"Me either," Stella replied. "I wonder what it's like over there."

"I wish you could come with me," Matilda groaned. "But I've got to do this on my own. I felt really strongly about that earlier. And now I'm scared to death by it."

Stella patted her arm. "You'll be fine. You're very capable. And besides, if you don't find any of your family, you can simply come back home. Right?"

"Right, I'll just fly home. It's no big deal."

"Nothing to worry about." Stella gave a nod. "Regardless, I still think you're mad, taking time off work, breaking up with your boyfriend—even if he is a jerk—and traveling to the other side of the world because of a DNA test."

"Maybe I *am* crazy. I don't know. Does a crazy person know if they're crazy? Or do they need other people to point it out?"

"You're not really crazy. I'd tell you if you were."

"You would? You're such a good sister." Matilda winked.

Stella's eyes twinkled. "I'd get you the best white jacket. All the other crazy people would be jealous."

Matilda laughed. "You'll stay in touch? Make sure I'm alive every few days?"

Stella's nostrils flared. "I'm already anxious enough. You don't have to make it worse. What if you die? I didn't even think of that. There won't be anyone over there looking out for you. You'll be all alone!" Stella's voice rose an octave as the realisation dawned.

Matilda couldn't help goading her. "And what if I die in a shoot-out? They have gangs over there. I could stray onto the wrong street. Will you fly over to collect my body and bring me home?"

Stella glared at her. "That's not even funny."

"I thought it was a little funny." Matilda reached for a sliced carrot and popped it into her mouth.

"You have a twisted sense of humour. You know how anxious I get."

"Sorry, sis. I promise not to cross into gang territory. And if I do, I'll make sure to wear the right coloured bandanna."

"It's not West Side Story," Stella sniffed.

"Maybe you're right. I guess I'll find out soon enough."

Chapter Eight

The Atlanta airport was a stark contrast to the one she'd left twenty-four hours earlier on the sunny Gold Coast. It was like a small city. Crowds jostled her onto a lightning-fast train that carried her to baggage claim. And once she'd collected her luggage, she lumbered outside into frigid weather and sleeting rain.

With a gasp, she set down her bags and foraged for a coat. She didn't have a waterproof one, but it was reasonably warm. Her raincoat was somewhere in the bottom of her suitcase, and she couldn't find it without upending the entire thing over the dirty footpath. Or sidewalk. She should probably get used to saying things the American way while she was here. She'd already struggled to communicate with waitresses, customs officers, and the man at the check-in counter in Los Angeles. No one seemed to be able to comprehend her accent. She'd have to work on that, or it would be a frustrating visit.

A man in a thin jumper and long, soiled pants approached her. His short hair curled tight against his dark skin. "Can I help with your bags?"

"Oh yes, thanks. That's very kind of you. I'm looking for a taxi."

He stared at her a moment with brow furrowed, then walked off, tugging her suitcase behind him. She watched in alarm before hurrying after him shouting. "Excuse me, where are you going with my suitcase?"

"You want a cab?" He called back over his shoulder.

"Yes, a cab. Thanks."

"That's some accent you've got."

She smiled. "I'm Australian."

"No kidding? *Put another shrimp on the barbie!*" he said with glee.

She frowned. "Huh?" Frozen rain fell on her head.

"Crocodile Dundee," he added as she ran to keep up with him. He glanced at her and waggled his eyebrows. "Right?"

"Oh yeah, right. Crocodile Dundee. He was great."

"I love that guy."

"Here you go. You can catch a cab here anywhere you like. That's twenty bucks."

"Twenty...?" She blinked. "I thought you were being kind ... never mind. Sure. Okay." She fished in her wallet for the money and handed it to him.

He shoved it in his pocket. "Enjoy Atlanta."

She nodded. "Thanks." So much for the kindness of strangers. She'd have to be more careful in the future, or she'd use up all her US currency in a week. She could've managed those few metres on her own.

The walk to the cab rank had passed through a patch of freezing rain and now her woollen jumper was soaked through. She stood in line behind dozens of other passengers, her hair plastered to her face. Her lips soon lost feeling. She shivered, her teeth knocking together. The longer she stood still in line, the colder she grew.

The internet had lied to her about *Hotlanta*. The sun was

hidden beyond a set of dark and brooding clouds. While she waited the frozen rain stopped falling, but the cold only intensified as darkness descended. And she became more and more miserable with every passing moment. Her stomach growled, and she felt sick from the travel. She hadn't slept more than a few minutes on the plane. She'd spent an entire day with no shower, eating airplane food and enjoying only a couple of brief, interrupted naps with her head tilted at a weird angle, leaving her neck with a stabbing pain every time she moved.

Finally, it was her turn for a taxi. She climbed in and gave the address for the bed and breakfast she'd booked. It was in Covington, which was the same town where Tyler Osbourne apparently lived. Although she wondered how up-to-date the information online was. Even thinking about him made her stomach jangle with nerves. What if she couldn't find him? Or if she did, what if he was a criminal or an axe murderer? That was probably the worst-case scenario. But she had a tendency to catastrophise when she was tired or anxious. And right now, she was both.

* * *

They'd been driving for almost two hours. It was dark. There hadn't been any more rain, for which Matilda was grateful. Although she was alarmed at the speed her driver managed on the highway, when the traffic allowed for it. Surely, the tarmac must be slick in this weather? Which probably explained why they were sitting in stop and go traffic and had been since they left the airport. The highway was massive with what seemed like at least a dozen lanes, and yet every single outgoing lane was at a standstill with no sign of improvement.

She leaned forward. "Are we almost there?"

She'd been watching the timer click over with her fare and this cab ride was going to cost her a fortune.

The driver had an accent and according to a badge on the visor, his name was Aarav. He gave a quick nod. "Not far now. You've come a long way?"

"Yes, from Australia."

He whistled. "That is far. I'm from India; we love to beat Australia in the cricket."

She chuckled. "You *wish* you could."

He grinned at her in the rearview mirror.

She was desperate to go to the toilet and her stomach growled with hunger. If she didn't stop before they reached the bed and breakfast, she wouldn't be able to eat a thing until the next morning. "Do you think we could stop at this shop up ahead, Aarav? I'm really hungry, and I don't have anything else with me."

"You want to stop?" He peered in the rearview mirror at her.

"Yes, please. Up here?" She pointed.

"Okay. Sure. We can take back roads the rest of the way. It will be better, no?" Then pulled into the petrol station, or gas station as the Americans called it. She'd have to start using the right vernacular. Already she could tell that people struggled to understand her accent and language. She was surprised by it. She didn't find it very difficult to understand them, but perhaps they hadn't heard many Australian accents while she'd watched American movies and television shows her entire life.

The ground was wet and slick when she climbed out. Her feet slipped out from under her, and she scrambled in place, able to keep her balance, but only just. Steadying herself with one hand on the car door, she breathed a sigh of relief and headed for the shop.

Inside, the tile floor was marked with muddy boot prints. She tip-toed around them and headed for the snack stands. After piling her arms full of snacks and drinks, most which she didn't recognise, she went to pay. There was a line, so she waited her turn. She'd always wanted to try a Twinkie, so she peeled one open and took a bite. It was delicious and she closed her eyes to better savour it as she chewed. Behind her, a man cleared his throat.

She opened her eyes to look at him, and he nodded at the counter. It was open. He was tall and handsome but watched her with narrowed eyes. He seemed irritated. She'd only delayed him by a few moments. Why were people so impatient? She offered him a tight smile and stepped forward to pay.

The cashier handed her snacks and drinks back to her in a small, plastic bag. Then she turned to leave, but her foot caught on the edge of a floor rug. She stumbled and righted herself just as she reached the slippery, wet tiles. With arms out and eyes wide, she felt her feet leave the floor and she went flailing backwards. One hand caught something as she fell, and she realised in horror it was the man who'd been impatiently waiting behind her. His coffee went flying, spraying across the front of his shirt before plummeting to the floor beside her and spilling across the tiles.

When she landed on her rear end, pain shot through her body. She grimaced and quickly scrambled to her feet. The man tried to help her, but she was too mortified to let him.

"Someone's had a few too many," said a deep voice behind her.

Her throat tightened. She was too tired for this. Too hungry. Too alone. "Well, I'm sorry," she snapped. "The floor is slippery."

The man's blue jacket was flecked with coffee. She handed him a napkin from her bag of snacks. "Here, this might help."

He grunted as he wiped at the flecks of coffee on his coat. "You in a hurry or somethin'?"

Her eyes narrowed, and she felt the sting of tears ache in her throat. "I am now." She stormed out of the shop, and back to the car, steaming mad, embarrassed and hurt. After climbing into the car, she slammed the door shut. "Let's go, Aarav."

He started the car in silence.

She couldn't believe what had just happened. The slip and fall wasn't the worst part of it. It was the way the man had treated her, as if he didn't care whether she was okay or not. His intense green eyes had sparkled in a way that made it seem as though he found some kind of perverse pleasure in her accident. What kind of person did that? Sure, he'd helped her to her feet, but he hadn't asked if she was okay. Perhaps he was angry about the coffee stains, although it didn't look as though he'd been burned, for which she was grateful. Things could've been so much worse. As it was, all she'd really suffered was some humiliation and a bruised derrière.

The Twinkie was ruined, no doubt smushed into the floor of the shop. But she dug through the bag for another treat and opened a Mountain Dew to wash it down with.

Fifteen minutes later, they pulled into the parking lot beside the bed and breakfast. Aarav helped her inside with her luggage and then left her to check in. It was a late check-in, so there was no one at the desk, only an envelope with her name waiting for her. The key was inside.

She lugged her things to room number three and unlocked the door. Once inside, she stripped out of her wet things and took a long, hot shower, before falling into bed with her bag of snacks. The journey hadn't started on the best terms, but things had to improve. Surely, the only way from here was up.

Chapter Nine

"What do you call a baby potato?" Amanda asked, as she leaned through the serving window at the cafe.

Rita placed an order in the queue and rolled her eyes. "I have no idea. What?"

"A small fry." Amanda's belly laugh resounded through the kitchen as she returned to her griddle and flipped each of the pancakes on it.

Rita huffed. "Bless your heart. Your sense of humour gets worse with age."

Amanda grinned at her. "You're just jealous. Admit it."

"I hope those pancakes are as soft as you are."

Amanda shot her a wink. "You know they are."

"And don't forget the bacon."

"I won't."

"You did last time."

"You're never going to let me forget that, are you? It was six months ago."

"Well..." Rita shook her head. "You know you can't live it down. Not with me."

"Elephant memory." Amanda grunted. "Bacon coming right up."

Rita marched out of the kitchen with a smile lingering on her face. There was a woman waiting at the door by the *Please wait to be seated* sign. She hurried to greet her. The place was packed, so she quickly scanned the cafe to see if she could spot an opening as she approached the woman. There was one small table by the window. So far, they'd managed with a first-come, first-served approach. But with the cafe's popularity growing since the Atlanta Journal called them a *Hidden Gem*, she figured it wouldn't be long before she'd have to change to a booking system with a computer and everything. It would drive her crazy, no doubt.

"Good morning, table for one?"

The woman nodded. "Yes, thanks."

"Follow me please."

After she'd seated the woman, she hurried back to the kitchen, her thoughts already elsewhere.

Meanwhile, Matilda watched the hostess from where she sat, working up the nerve to say something. To ask, *do you know Rita Osbourne? Who is she? Where is she? And how about Tyler? Does he live around here?* But she hadn't been given a chance by the woman who seated her. She'd rushed off the moment Matilda reached the table. And now the waitress serving tables nearby wasn't making eye contact, her gaze firmly planted on the notepad in her hands as she scribbled down orders.

The cafe was charming. A slightly crooked blue and white sign hung above the doorway that read, *The Honeysuckle Cafe.* There was a vine draped across the sign that ran all the way down to the ground on both sides. It looked dead but was probably honeysuckle lying dormant for the winter. Matilda didn't know much about honeysuckle, but she imagined it was pretty during summer.

All around her hummed conversations in thick southern accents. Heat pumped from vents and the room was furnished with small round tables, blue and white checked tablecloths and mismatched chairs.

The scent of frying bacon filled the air. Matilda had eaten a light breakfast already, but the scents were so delightful, she couldn't resist ordering a plate of poached eggs, bacon, and hotcakes when the waitress came to the table. She also opted for an enormous cappuccino, since her jet lag was making her feel as though she was sleepwalking.

She enjoyed people-watching through the window while she waited for her meal. Covington was set around a square with the cafe on one corner. The old buildings that hugged the square were regal, red brick with white trim. There was a clock tower on one. And columns on another. A large grassy park filled the centre of the square. The grass was yellow and sodden from the rain overnight.

People hurried by with umbrellas at their side. Cars crawled around the square. And inside the cafe, diners came and went. It was a Saturday, and some were seated around a leisurely breakfast. Others popped through the door, setting the bell jangling, to pick up a takeout order, or a to-go coffee. Everyone seemed to know the hostess. She was middle-aged or slightly older. It was hard to say. But her hair was tinged with grey, her face was lined, and she had a big smile for each customer who she called by name.

One of the takeout customers called out "Bye now, Rita." He waved and left with his bag of food.

Matilda's eyes widened. The hostess was Rita. Now all she had to do was find an opportunity to speak to her again. Her food arrived, and she took a bite of the eggs on sourdough. The yolk burst across her tongue, the bread was soft and delicious.

She sipped her cappuccino and then called Stella.

"Hello, sister," she said.

Stella shouted with delight. "Why did you wait so long to call me? It's late here. Did you get there okay?"

Matilda laughed and took another sip of coffee. It burned her tongue. She grimaced. "I arrived last night, and I'm at the cafe having brunch. It's really quaint. And the food is delicious."

"That sounds great. Listen, your work called and they're wondering what to do with Solomon."

Solomon was an aging Dalmatian who regularly came in for dental work but wouldn't let anyone touch him other than Matilda.

"He loves cheese. Tell them to give him some cheese and he'll warm up in no time."

"Okay, I'll do that. How's your hotel?"

"I'm staying at this really lovely, country-style bed and breakfast. I can't tell you how happy I was to fall into the extremely comfortable bed last night. The flight was a shocker. I've never felt so tired and greasy in all my life. That first shower was ecstasy."

Stella laughed. "I'll take your word for it. Any hot men in that part of the world?"

"Why are you asking me about men?" Matilda asked.

"You're single now, you need to find someone."

"We're taking some time apart and we're going to talk about our relationship when I get back. I'm not sure if that qualifies as single."

"I don't mean to be rude, but that sounds lame," Stella said with a huff.

Matilda gaped. "That is rude. I can't believe you said that."

"Well, come on. You've been dating for two years. He should've popped the question by now, or be working up to it, at the very least. And he wants time and space away from you? Not to mention the awful things he said. I think you should find someone amazing and fall head over heels in love. You'll forget about Cam in no time."

"I'm not looking for a relationship. Definitely not. It's the absolute last thing on my mind."

"Sometimes it happens when you're not looking."

"There are some cute guys here, though. If I was looking, which I'm not. I ran into one last night, literally. He was kind of a jerk. But very good-looking."

"Sounds like a *mark and avoid* type of situation. I like your initiative though. Keep it up."

When Matilda hung up the phone, she immediately missed her sister and wished she'd asked her to come along for the journey. She felt very alone. She shook it off and continued eating her brunch, while scrolling on her phone for things to do in Covington.

There seemed to be a lot of supernatural type tours, something she was not the slightest bit interested in. She had no desire to return to the dark and historic bed and breakfast alone after a long day of spooky stories. Other than a couple of restaurants, which she bookmarked, there didn't seem to be much else to do. At least there was always the good shopping to look forward to—she'd heard that the shopping in the USA was fantastic and she'd purposely packed light in order to take advantage of it.

Rita led a couple to the table next to hers. Matilda quickly raised a hand. "Excuse me?"

Rita met her gaze with a chirpy blue-eyed smile. "Can I help?"

Matilda stood, clasping her hands together. "Yes, is your name Rita Osbourne?"

"Yes, Ma'am."

"That's great, because I need to talk to you about something."

* * *

By the time Matilda had finished telling Rita her story, the older woman had found her way into the seat opposite her with a look of confusion on her face.

"So you're somehow related to Tyler Osbourne?"

"Yes, that's what the DNA test results produced when I fed them into the website. I'm trying to find out who Tyler is. Do you know anyone by that name?"

"Not off the top of my head," Rita replied, her brow furrowed. "But I have a quick question—how could you be related to him? Do you know?"

Matilda inhaled a deep breath. "No, I don't. I'm really not sure. The website indicated he was a cousin of mine, but I don't see how that's possible. My parents have passed, but when they were alive, they never said anything about having family over here. If he's my cousin, that would mean one of them must've had a sister or brother living in this country. My uncle did visit here, but he never said anything about having a child. And to add to that, my DNA results showed I wasn't related to either of my parents. So, I'm very confused. Because my Auntie said that she saw me born."

"That's a complicated story. Something's not adding up," Rita replied. "What are your folks names? Maybe I know them."

"John and Daphne Berry. They're from Kingscliff in New South Wales."

Rita shook her head. "They don't sound familiar."

"Hmm... I was hoping you might have known them at some point. This is going to be trickier than I thought."

"Listen, honey, I've got a crowd to feed and they're getting restless. But I don't want to brush you off."

"Thanks, I've come a long way..."

"How about you give me your number and I'll call you?

We can talk." Rita's eyes crinkled around the edges as she smiled.

"Thanks, I'd like that. I'm back to square one, I guess. I've got to track down Tyler. And I have no idea where to start. I'd hoped you might know him, given you live in Covington and he shares your surname. But now I don't know what to do. I suppose I could visit the courthouse, see if there are any records there."

"Oh, they have all that online these days. You don't have to go and do all that." Rita waved a hand. "We'll figure it out. I'm glad to help. Let's catch up soon."

Chapter Ten

TWENTY-SEVEN YEARS AGO

The military plane landed with a puff of dust around its wheels. Helen Brown's heart leapt inside her chest. She'd waited for this moment for six long months, and it was finally here. *He* was finally here. Her husband, Paul, was deployed to Kenya. He'd been gone a whole year with one trip home halfway through that stint. And he still had three years left to go. She wasn't sure if she was going to make it that long. Him being gone was the hardest thing she'd ever had to face before in her life. Every day felt like a trial. It was easier now than it'd been at first, but it still hurt all the time. She pined for their next video chat, waited for the email messages to load with bated breath. Couldn't stand waiting for his next visit, but all of that was pushed out of her thoughts in the moment as she watched him descend the steps onto the tarmac.

The wind whipped at her straw hat, and she pressed a hand to hold it in place as she ran across the tarmac towards him. Her floral dress flapped around her legs. She was conscious that she likely looked childish—the other women with their children stood back waiting patiently. But not her. She couldn't wait another moment to be in his arms. She leapt at him, wrapping one leg around him as she laughed against his searching lips. He kissed her long and hard, his arms tightly pulling her to him by the waist. Then whispered, "Baby, I've missed you."

She grinned. "More than anything in the world?"

"Yes, more than anything."

"Me too," she said, her forehead pressed to his so that their eyes were fixed upon one another.

They walked back to the car together. He had one arm around her waist, the other holding his backpack in place over his shoulder. She couldn't stop grinning and every now and then leaned over to kiss whatever part of him she could reach.

He laughed at her, put his backpack down on the road behind the car, then placed one of his hands on each of her cheeks. He gazed into her eyes with longing, then leaned forward to kiss her soft and long on the mouth.

By the time he pulled away, she was dizzy.

"I've been waiting so long for you, husband."

"Well, here I am, wife. What are you going to do with me?"

She laughed and hurried to climb into the car while he loaded his bag in the back. "Oh, I can think of a few things."

* * *

After they'd made love for hours, Helen lay in Paul's arms with a contented smile. She twirled her fingers around his, letting her cheek rest on his chest.

"I've got your whole stay planned out," she said. "We can go to Krispy Kreme, then I thought we might have dinner at Mary Mac's with the rest of the family."

"Is every day going to revolve around food?" he asked, one eyebrow quirked.

She pouted. "Maybe."

"Because I'm good with that." He laughed. "Although I want to spend time with you too. Don't schedule too much."

She kissed his chest. "I promise. Lots of time with me."

"How are Mom and Dad doing?"

She shrugged. "I told them you get in tomorrow morning. I wanted to have the entire evening with you by myself."

He groaned. "You're gonna get me in trouble."

"They can have you all to themselves in the morning. I want tonight."

"Are you hungry?" he asked. "Because I'm starving."

"Pizza?" she asked.

He nodded. "That would be perfect. And could we watch a game? I don't even know what's on."

"We'll just have to figure it out. I'll order the pizza."

"I'm going to jump in the shower," he replied, climbing out of bed.

She watched him walk to the shower, her throat constricting with unshed tears. It was so good to have him back. She wanted him to stay, but she knew it was impossible.

"Don't forget we have to see my parents too. They've invited us for a BBQ on Saturday at the lake," she called after him.

He turned the shower on, letting the water heat up and steam rose towards the ceiling. "Okay, but your Dad has to be nice. I'm not sixteen anymore, he can't keep treating me like I am."

She sighed. "He's still angry with you for dating me."

"But I married you."

"Yes, you did. And he's never quite forgiven you." She laughed. "I'm only joking. Dad loves you ... really. He's just gruff. That's his style. I don't think he can change at this point, he's too old."

Paul shook his head. "I know, but for once it would be nice if he'd act as though he likes me. At least a little bit."

"I'll talk to him."

"No ... don't do that. He'll call me whiny again."

Her lips pursed. She loved it when her father and husband got along, but it was a rare event. They'd been hunting together once and went on two fishing trips. All three outings had been a success. But as soon as they were back in the city, her Dad acted like Paul was that sixteen-year-old boy knocking on the door to take her out all over again.

"He'll be good. I promise."

Paul grinned at her. "And I'll suck up to him like I always do. Anything for you, baby."

Chapter Eleven

Through the window, a blue jay bobbed on a branch. There were no leaves. The sky was a grey colour, and although it was toasty warm in her room, a shiver ran through Matilda's body as she looked at the frost-covered grass outside. The bird fascinated Matilda. She'd never seen a blue jay before, but she'd googled it the moment she saw it since it was beautiful. Its plumage was brilliant in contrast to the grey landscape. It was larger than she'd thought it would be, and when it flew off, she was disappointed to see it go.

She hugged herself in the soft bathrobe provided by the bed and breakfast and then padded across the thick carpet to the bathroom. She turned on the shower and waited, but nothing happened. No water, not a drop. She'd had a shower without any issue the previous evening, but now she couldn't get it to work. She turned the handle back again, then forward. Again, the shower remained dry.

With hands on her hips, she stared at the shower for a few moments, then went to the bed and sat before picking up the phone to call reception. She reported the issue with the shower, then lay on the bed to watch the news while she waited for the promised handyman to come to her room.

She didn't know what to make of Rita. The woman had seemed very friendly, had come across warm and open. But she was hiding something. It seemed as though she'd closed off when Matilda mentioned Tyler. It could be in Matilda's imagination. She might be making it all up. But it was a feeling she had, one she couldn't quite explain.

Another thing on her mind was the issue with Cam. Well, not exactly. What really bothered her was that it didn't bother her. Which was silly, when she thought about it. But why wasn't she thinking about him every moment of the day? Why wasn't she heartbroken that he'd asked for space? She should've been mourning the loss. He hadn't called or texted, hadn't checked in with her, sent an email or photo. They'd had a few close calls in the past when she'd almost ended things between them, and he'd bombarded her with romantic gestures or poetry via text messages, begging her to give them another chance because they belonged together.

And now, nothing. She had told him she needed to think and he should stop harassing her. But Cam never listened to anyone.

Even though that should offend her, it didn't. She felt almost a sense of relief. Which made her even more despondent because that meant it was time to move on. If she wasn't upset about things ending between them, then they shouldn't reconnect when she returned to Australia. It wasn't working out. He wasn't her soul mate, and if she was honest with herself, she'd known that for a long time. She'd let their relationship continue because it was easier than confronting him to end things. He hadn't wanted to move on, had always clung to her like she was his life raft, and she'd let him because it was nice to be needed, to be wanted.

With a sigh, she flicked through the channels, looking for something to watch but not really wanting to get into anything deep. She found a news channel and left it there, letting the reporters' voices sooth her while she returned to her thoughts.

She was soon interrupted by a knock at the door. Gathering her robe around her, she tightened the tie around her waist and hurried to open it. When she saw him standing on the threshold, she gasped audibly.

It was the tall man from the petrol station.

"You?" she asked.

He frowned. "Coffee lady?"

"What are you doing here?" Nerves fluttered in her stomach followed by a stern indignation. She raised her chin.

"I'm here to fix the shower? You called the desk and said it wasn't working."

"Oh? You're the handyman?"

He nodded, eyes glinting with delight at the situation. Of course he was enjoying it, she was uncomfortable and that made him happy. "Ryan Merritt, at your disposal."

"Thanks for your promptness. I'm Matilda Berry, come with me. I'll show you to the shower." She spun on her heel.

"I know where the shower is," he replied with a chuckle.

"Of course." She stepped aside. She followed him into the bathroom. Why did she always act so proper and formal when she was irritated? She pronounced every word precisely, even as anxiety clustered around a rapid heartbeat in her chest. She didn't know why he made her so uncomfortable, but he just had to fix the shower and then he would leave and she wouldn't have to see him ever again.

He stepped up to the shower and leaned down to press something below the tap, then turned the lever and water spurted out. He moved away, scratched his head. "Looks fine to me. What seems to be the problem?"

Embarrassment flooded through her. "Uh ... sorry. I didn't know about that button thingy."

"Right, well, you've got to press the button first, then the water comes out."

She wanted to slap herself on the forehead, but he already thought she was stupid. There was no need to confirm it for him.

"I haven't seen that before. I'm not sure how I made it work the first time."

He shrugged. "It's not very common. There are a thousand different types of faucets. This one tricks a lot of folks. Sometimes the button stays stuck."

She crossed her arms. "Well, thanks."

"No problem. Since neither one of us is holding hot coffee, I think we'll get through it unscathed this time." He strode back to the front door.

She frowned. "You know, that was an accident. The floor was slick."

"Oh, I get it. You're not from 'round here, are you?"

"No, but I don't see how that's relevant."

"A local would've known the floor was slick. You didn't even slow down." His eyes narrowed. "What kind of an accent is that anyway? British?"

"No, I'm Australian," she said, indignant at his mistake. She wasn't sure why. Maybe it was his whole demeanour—tall, handsome, smug, rude. He had a vibe she didn't like. It made her want to squirm with irritation.

"You're a long way from home."

She waited for another snide remark, but it didn't come.

"Well, thanks again."

"You're welcome. Call the desk if you have any other problems. I'm here for another hour or so."

She shut the door behind him, confused. He seemed to like teasing her at every opportunity, had been rude multiple times, and yet hadn't poked fun about the shower incident and offered to help with anything else she needed. He also smelled really good. She leaned against the door and inhaled slowly, his aftershave still clinging to the air around her. What was that smell? Whatever it was, she liked it. Cam wore a kind of fruity scent that made her nose itch, and she always felt a little sick whenever he overdid it. But this scent was masculine, warm and rich, without being overpowering.

She yawned wide, then headed for the bathroom. It was time for a shower and then she was going to bed. It was early, but she couldn't stay up any later. The jetlag was killing her.

The shower switched on easily now that she knew about the button. She stepped into the stream of warm water, wondering at how much more luxurious showers were here than at home—such a heavy stream of water.

It was already dark outside, and she'd skipped dinner since she was too tired to face going out and didn't have anything in her room that would qualify. She'd make up for it with a big breakfast in the morning. And hopefully, when she caught up on her sleep, she could figure out her next move. Because right now, she was at a dead end. Returning home to Brisbane without having discovered anything about her biological family wasn't an option.

Chapter Twelve

TWENTY-SEVEN YEARS AGO

The rhythmic pounding of her feet on the treadmill was soothing in a strange kind of way. Helen enjoyed running. It was one of the few pleasures she allowed herself these days. Between work, taking care of her parents (although they very much dismissed the fact that she needed to do anything of the sort) and church, she was busy enough that she could easily skip the occasional leg day or stint on the treadmill. But it was her gym sessions that kept her going, gave her the energy to face the busyness of her life.

She'd spent the day working as a nurse in the maternity wing of Piedmont Hospital. And even though she was tired, it invigorated her to finish her day at the gym.

Besides, going home to an empty house wasn't particularly appealing.

Helen glanced up at the television screen hanging above the line of treadmills and elliptical machines. The noise of running feet, the ding of notifications, and the buzz of conversation drowned out the quiet television set. She couldn't hear what they were saying. She could guess though. Pictures flashed across the screen—another bombing in Kenya. What was going on over there? It was supposed to be a peacekeeping mission. That's what they'd been told. But the fighting was still going on over a year later, and they seemed no closer to peace.

She didn't want to know if it was near where her husband was stationed. She'd spent too many sleepless nights worrying about him now that he was back in Africa.

They'd had such a wonderful time together over the four weeks of his leave. They'd eaten out at all his favourite restaurants, spent time with friends and family, and driven to North Georgia, the Smoky Mountains, to stay in a log cabin with a deliciously relaxing hot tub on the porch. Every waking moment had been with him. She'd taken leave from work to cherish their time together. But it had all come to an end far too soon, and now he was gone, back to his work and out of her life.

It was for the best, that's what she kept telling herself. After he finished his term with the army, he'd be able to go to school. It would set them up for life. Them and the family they planned to have. It was what they both dreamed of. Neither she nor Paul needed anything fancy. Just a home in the suburbs they could call their own, and children to fill the rooms with laughter and love.

Tuition paid for by the army was the first step in their plan. It would allow Paul to become an engineer, something he'd dreamed of since he was a little boy. He'd be the first in his family to attend college, if he made it. Which he would, she was certain of that. When Paul put his mind to something, he made it happen. The scholarship would help them get the start in life they needed. But she was beginning to wonder if the cost was worth it. Four years apart, four years as newlyweds spent in different parts of the world.

After a year, it was already beginning to eat at her. And they still had three years left to go. Every time she caught a glimpse of the news bulletin out of the corner of her eye, her heart skipped a beat and the ball of anxiety in her stomach grew.

She purposely looked away, squeezed her eyes shut and focused on counting her footsteps, breathing deeply in through her nose and out through her mouth.

What if he died? What would she do then? She couldn't think about it.

Had to keep moving forward. They were trying for a baby. They'd talked about it when he visited and decided it was time.

If she had a baby, maybe she'd be able to focus on something else other than the loneliness in her chest. But how could she raise a child without a father? She'd told him they should wait until he came home for good, but he said there was no harm in trying now. He was impatient, wanted to get started on filling those bedrooms.

"But we don't have a house yet. Only a rental," she'd objected.

He'd laughed at that. "It's a matter of time. You grow the baby, and I'll grow our nest egg."

Helen lifted some weights, pushing herself for one more rep, heavier weights, to keep going, to feel the pain. Anything other than focusing on the ache in her heart. She'd never realised how much being apart could feel like grief until now.

The pain of missing her husband was all-consuming. Knowing he could die thousands of miles from home and she would never see him again ate away at her. She tried not to let it, and most of the time, she managed to keep her chin up and a smile on her face. Most people she knew wouldn't realise the strain it placed on her, having him so far away and in constant danger. But sometimes the fear crept in.

After stretching, she marched to the locker room. She undressed and wrapped herself in a towel to head for the showers. Halfway there she reconsidered, returned to her locker and fetched a pregnancy test. She unwrapped it as she walked back to the toilet stalls. Paul had been back on duty for a month. She might be pregnant, and if she was, it could show up on the test. It would be early, but it was possible. Some good news might lift her spirits.

She waited the two minutes it took for the little pink lines to appear, but there was only one. She wasn't pregnant. Her heart fell.

When they'd first started talking about having a baby, she'd been scared. They weren't ready. A baby would change everything. They were newlyweds. They should wait. Spend some time together as a couple. Go on a few trips. Enjoy their freedom. But now, a year later, he was ready even if she wasn't quite sure about the timing.

Her main concern was doing it alone. Paul had argued that if she fell pregnant now even with him out of the country, she'd have plenty of support with both sets of parents nearby. It didn't matter that he wasn't around. The baby was too little to notice. And besides, how could they have four kids if they didn't start soon? She wasn't sure she was capable of it. Any of it. Especially the four kids.

But it didn't matter because she wasn't pregnant.

After she'd showered, she drove to her parents' lake house. Her sister, Rita, and Rita's husband, Jimmy, lived there with them. The younger couple at one end of the house with their two small children, the parents at the other.

Rita and Jimmy were saving for their own home. At least that's what they told everyone. Although they didn't seem to be in any hurry. They'd lived there for years, had two children, and made no mention of moving out.

Helen couldn't blame them. Her parents were loving and

kind. And the lake house was spacious, beautiful, and had a special place in her heart since it was where Rita and Helen grew up. Her father had inherited the property from his parents. And he'd told Rita he intended to leave it to her as the eldest child. Helen wanted to be magnanimous about it but couldn't help feeling a little jealous since she'd had no control over when she was born.

She pulled into the driveway and parked her car. A small scruffy dog bounded out to greet her and instantly rolled onto his back. She bent to scratch his belly.

"Hello, Ronald," she said in a sing-song voice. "Have you been a good boy?"

The dog wagged his tail, pink tongue lolling from the side of his mouth. Floppy black and white fur fell across his eyes, and she pushed it clear with one hand. "How on earth can you see where you're going? I need to get you a hairband."

Ronald always made her feel better and brought a smile to her face. Dogs had a way of doing that. The lake had a similar effect. She straightened, pressed her hands to the small of her back and looked out across the water. It was dark now, mid-summer. The scent of freshly cut grass, the sound of water lapping at the docks, the glow of the full moon on the water's surface—all of it was so familiar. She'd spent many hours seated on the edge of the dock with her feet dangling into the water, a fishing pole in one hand. It was her sanctuary. Her quiet place.

Inside the lake house she found Rita playing the piano. Mum stood beside the piano, arms aloft and mouth wide, mid-song. Her strong alto voice soared, and Helen itched to join in, but she hadn't inherited her mother's musical ability the way Rita had.

Mom's face was scrunched in the ecstasy of the moment. There was nothing she liked more than the drama and emotion of a good song. She always said it drew her in until she lived on each note. She'd taught them both to play the piano, but only Rita had carried it on.

Helen wasn't much interested in music. She enjoyed it, but it wasn't a passion for her the way it was for her mother and sister. Her focus was animals. She adored them.

If she could, she'd adopt every one she could find and keep them as pets. She wished she had space to keep a whole menagerie of them. But for now, she and Paul rented a small cottage on the base. And there was nowhere to keep a pet. It would be cruel.

One day, she'd fill the house with them, and with babies too, if she was lucky and Paul got his way. With him gone, she wanted to shout that she'd give him anything he liked in all the world, if only he'd come home. But there was nothing to be done about that.

"Hi Mom," she said, leaning in to kiss her mother's cheek.

Mom stopped singing mid-word. "Where have you been and why is your hair all wet?"

"Hello, Rita." She bent to kiss her sister's cheek. "You smell nice. Like chocolate fudge. I took a shower after working out."

Rita laughed. "Good nose! I've been trying out new recipes all day."

"Where's Dad?" Helen asked.

"He's fixing the boat." Mum rolled her eyes. "As usual."

"Let's hope he doesn't drop any more tools in the water," Helen replied.

Rita laughed.

"Has he been to see the cardiologist lately?"

Mum's smile faded. "You know Dad. He thinks he'll be fine. I'm making a fuss about nothing."

Helen shook her head. "Mum, you've got to make him go. It's important."

Mum reached up to cup Helen's cheek the way she had

when Helen was a child. "I know, honey, I'm trying. Meanwhile, what would you like to eat for dinner? You're staying for dinner, aren't you? I was thinking ... chicken and dumplings."

Helen smiled. "I love chicken and dumplings."

Rita closed the piano, and they both followed their mother into the kitchen. Rita helped her with the dinner while Helen set the table, then sat down to do a crossword puzzle in the back of the newspaper. They chattered away while they worked. After a while, the back door swung open, and she heard her dad stamping his boots outside. He kicked them off and padded into the kitchen in his socks.

"Hey, Dad, how's the boat?"

He removed his hat and set it on a peg. "The darned thing just won't start."

"Never mind, Dad, you'll get it working tomorrow," said Helen.

He grunted. "Hello, hon, what are you doing here? Come on over here and hug my neck."

She stood to give him a hug. "Thought I'd come for some chicken and dumplings."

"Ah, your mother is stealing the cafe's recipe again, is she?"

"You know full well I use grandma's recipe just like you do," Mum declared with flashing eyes.

Helen laughed at their constant sparring. "How's the old place going?"

She sat next to her sister, wrapped one arm around Rita's shoulders as she answered her. "The cafe is doing fine. Right, Dad?"

"Right, Pumpkin," he said.

"We hired a new manager. I'm hoping that will help cut back on my hours a little bit so I can spend more time with the kids. Are you coming in tomorrow, Dad?"

He shrugged. "Not sure you need me there. Thought I

might go fishing, if I can get this dang boat started. I'm not feeling the best at the moment. You think you can manage without me?"

She nodded. "Of course, you should take care of yourself."

"Go see that doctor Mum's been nagging you to see, then." Helen said, before popping a chip into her mouth and crunching it loudly.

He rolled his eyes. "Don't you start. I'm surrounded by hens, just peck, peck, pecking."

"We just want you to look after yourself, Dad," Rita said.

Helen chimed in. "You know she's right. Can I make the booking for you tomorrow?"

He threw his hands in the air. "What chance do I have? I'm surrounded. Fine, Helen, you can make the appointment, and I'll go and see the doctor if it gets the three of you to leave me alone."

He stomped out of the room. The women all looked at each other and broke into laughter.

"He's getting grouchier in his old age," Rita said.

Mum spooned dumplings into the soup. "Leave your father alone, girls. He's outnumbered and doesn't like being forced into anything. Let's change the subject. Helen, how's Paul? Have you heard from him lately?"

Tears sprang to her eyes. She hated for people to see her cry. She didn't want them to pity her. It made her feel weak. "He's fine. I spoke to him last night. I don't think he's thrilled to be back in Kenya. Of course he'd never say that, but I can read between the lines. I told him he has to stay safe for me, for all of us. That's his priority, to come home."

Mum patted her on the back sympathetically. "That's right, honey. And he'll be home before you know it. These few years will fly by. You'll see."

Unable to hold back the tears any longer, Helen busied

herself with her crossword puzzle, pretending to struggle with one of the answers.

Rita sat at the table across from her with a sigh. "Any luck with the you-know-what?" She exchanged a look with Helen whose eyes were still blurred with tears.

Helen quickly shook her head. "Not pregnant," she mouthed, so their mother wouldn't hear.

Rita's face clouded with sympathy. She shook her head, reached out a hand to squeeze Helen's. Mouthed back, "I'm sorry."

Rita and her lovely and supportive husband, Jimmy, had what seemed to be an idyllic life. And sometimes Helen couldn't help being jealous of her big sister. But more than that, she was happy for her.

"What are you two whispering about?" Mum asked.

Helen wiped her eyes with the back of her hand. "I took a pregnancy test at the gym. It was negative."

Mum placed a bowl in front of her and squeezed her shoulder. "Next time, honey, next time. These things can take a little while. Some people get pregnant first try and others take years, but you'll get there."

"What if there's something wrong with me?" Helen asked. "What if I can't get pregnant?"

Mum carried two more bowls to the table. "I'm sure you can and you will. Let's cross that bridge when we get to it. Besides, there are other options, you know."

Rita spoke up. "You could adopt or do IVF."

"I don't know," Helen replied. "I've thought about adopting, of course I have, but it sounds like such a long and expensive process."

"Well, it's something to think about anyway," Rita said.

"Yeah, I'll do that, but not until Paul's back. I was honestly a little bit relieved. He wants so badly for us to have a family right now, but I'd rather wait until he's home for good."

Dad joined them for dinner, and they all said grace together. They chatted about the cafe, the weather, the boat, and what they each planned to do for the coming weekend. But all Helen could think about was that pregnancy test and her husband so far away, unable to talk to him whenever she wanted, unable to ask for his advice, unable to feel his arms around her when she needed him the most. Would they ever have the family they dreamed of? Would they ever have the happiness they'd longed for? Since he'd shipped out soon after the wedding, they'd never really had the chance to be newly-weds. What would it be like to live in the same city day after day as a married couple, as a family? She only wished they could start now.

Chapter Thirteen

Three days had passed since Matilda visited the cafe and spoke to Rita. She'd spent that time exploring Covington, even caught an Uber to downtown Atlanta and had a look around at the World of Coca-Cola, the Underground Mall, and the famous Georgia Aquarium. She kept herself busy focusing on sightseeing and trying out the local cuisine, which she loved.

She'd eaten every type of vegetable imaginable in a casserole or fried. She'd had Brunswick stew and fried chicken and hot wings tossed in buffalo sauce served with celery and blue cheese dressing. But all the while, a single thought niggled at her mind, at the back of her mind.

What was she going to do now? She'd conducted a few Google searches. She'd called the vital records office. But she hadn't been able to locate Tyler Osborne.

There were so many people with that name all over the United States. It was far too common for her to narrow it down, and when she put Covington into the search box, she didn't find anything current. Whoever Tyler Osborne was, there was no way for her to pinpoint him on social media or with search engines. There were dozens in the state of Georgia alone, and she knew nothing else about him that would help her narrow the search results. She was about to admit defeat and plan a trip to Disney World when Rita called.

Her southern drawl echoed down the phone line.

"Well, hey there, this is Rita Osborne from the Honeysuckle Cafe."

"Hi, Rita, how nice to hear your voice." Why was Rita calling? Matilda cleared her throat. "Do you have a lead on Tyler Osborne?"

Rita hesitated. "Yeah, about that. We do need to talk, but not over the phone. How would you like to come to see a famous Georgia landmark on Sunday and have a picnic with my family? We can talk there."

"That sounds amazing, I would love that."

"Great, where are you staying?"

"I'm at the Greenfields Bed and Breakfast," Matilda replied.

"Ah yes, I know the place well. A friend of mine owns it. I'll pick you up after lunch."

"Really? Wow, it's a beautiful building," Matilda replied. "So historic with all that trim, and the grounds are incredible. Your friend is very lucky."

"He does okay, although you'd never know it to look at him. He's one of those folks who find luck wherever they go. Everything he touches turns to gold, you could say. And to top it all off, he's a nice guy."

"So, where are we going?" Matilda asked.

"I'm taking you to Stone Mountain, so wear comfortable shoes. And something warm. It's a beautiful day, the sun is shining, and with all the rain we've had this past week, everyone wants to get outside even though it's cold out, so bundle up."

"Sounds good to me. I love a picnic. And we Aussies never let a bit of weather stop us from getting out and about."

* * *

On Sunday Matilda dressed warmly. As promised, soon after lunch Rita arrived to pick her up. She drove a beat-up old Chevy truck and wore a knitted red hat pulled down low around her ears. Her greying curls sprung up around the hat like kudzu, a vine Matilda had recently learned about from the bed and breakfast manager. It covered the ground and other vegetation around the building, like an, all-consuming carpet of brown. Apparently it would be green when summer hit. But for now it looked dead.

As she strode down the footpath to the curb, she noticed Ryan tackling the kudzu with a buzzing weed eater. He glanced up at her, but she looked away, chin high. She wouldn't give him the satisfaction of acknowledging him. He didn't deserve her attention. Besides, she was embarrassed about the shower. What kind of ninny doesn't know how to operate a shower? Apparently, she was exactly that kind of ninny. And she hated that he knew that humiliating fact about her.

She climbed into Rita's truck, using the handle above the door to lift herself high enough to make it. She still wasn't used to how enormous vehicles were in this country.

With a grunt, she fixed her seat belt. "Good morning."

"Morning, honey." Rita shifted her position so she could see Ryan through the window, then waved vigorously.

Ryan dipped his head hello but continued working.

"Ugh, he's so annoying," Matilda said, purposely facing forward.

Rita studied her with a smile. "Is that so? What did he do?"

Matilda crossed her arms. "Never mind, it's not worth talking about."

"He might be annoying, but he sure is easy on the eyes." Rita laughed as she pulled away from the curb.

"I hadn't noticed."

Rita gave her sideeye. "Oh, really?"

"He's not my type." Matilda was adamant.

Rita laughed again. "Okay, I gotcha."

"So, where are we going again?"

"It's called Stone Mountain. I would explain, but that's really all it is. It's a stone ... that's a mountain. Anyway, it's got picnic tables and such. The family will all be set up when we get there. All you have to do is relax."

"This is your side of the family we're meeting?"

"They're a mixture. Osbournes and Browns."

Matilda's heart skipped a beat. Maybe someone there would know Tyler. It was a long shot but worth asking.

"You had any luck with your investigation yet?"

Matilda sighed. "No, nothing yet."

The picnic tables were located at the base of the mountain. It really was quite an impressive landmark. Matilda stared up at the rock face ahead of her with the figures of three military men on horseback carved into it. She didn't recognise any of the group, but she figured they had something to do with the civil war. Overhead, the sky was clear blue with a few fluffy white clouds. It had warmed up a lot since her arrival, and she almost didn't need her coat, although there was still a light breeze.

A group of people were gathered around a pair of picnic tables, and Rita and Matilda made their way over to them. Rita carried a picnic basket on one arm with a red and white checked cloth covering it. She set it on one of the tables. Everyone rushed to greet them both with embraces and exclamations of welcome.

"How lovely to meet you!"

"Let me hug your neck."

"Oh, bless your heart, you came a long way!"

Matilda tried to remember all of their names, but there were so many and they all looked far too much alike. There was Susan, Marie, Janet, Sean, Ron, Cathy, David, and Myra. Those were the ones she could recall, even if she wasn't able to put a face to each name. In all, there were around thirty people at the gathering. Several children ran about the place, squealing and chasing one another. It was Sunday, so the picnic area was well-populated by families with food, footballs, and frisbees.

"Did you say your name is Matilda?" one woman asked, sidling up to her.

She nodded. "That's right. And you're..." Matilda did her best to remember, but she couldn't manage to come up with a name for the earnest blonde woman with heavily made-up face standing in front of her.

"I'm Cathy. Don't you worry one little bit, we don't expect you to remember every single name right away. It's a big group. I know it can be overwhelming."

"Thanks," Matilda replied. "I'll try, but I'm not great with names."

"Rita didn't tell us much, but mentioned you were here looking for a family connection?"

"That's right. I'm trying to find Tyler Osbourne. Apparently, he's my cousin, although no one seems to know where he is. You don't know anyone by that name, do you?"

The woman offered a warm smile. "Well, how about that? A long-lost cousin. What an exciting mystery. And I love your accent, by the way."

"Well, thanks. I love yours too."

"Let me ask you something."

"Okay."

Cathy scooted closer to Matilda, holding a Starbucks cup aloft in one hand. "Do y'all have coffee out there in Australia? Because I don't know how I could survive without my coffee." She laughed loudly.

Matilda blinked. "Uh ... yeah, we have coffee."

"Well, thank goodness for that." Cathy took a big swig of coffee.

As she watched the woman saunter away, Matilda noted that Cathy hadn't actually answered her question.

And the rest of the picnic proceeded in much the same way. They ate fried chicken from Publix buckets with corn on the cob smothered in butter, potato salad, baked beans, and bread rolls. And every time Matilda got chatting with another member of the family, they were kind, welcoming, and completely avoided answering her questions about whether there was any family connection to Tyler or if they'd heard of him.

Frustrated, Matilda decided to join a group of the younger members of the family in climbing the mountain. They had to go around to the right hand side of the horseriders engraved in the stone face and make their way up with a crowd of other hikers. It wasn't a difficult climb and was quicker than she'd anticipated. The view from the top was incredible—they were so high up they could see a long way across the city. Atlanta was a large and sprawling metropolis. There were strip malls, highways, and suburban neighbourhoods as far as the eye could see in every direction.

She was suddenly overwhelmed by the enormity of what she was doing. She had flown to the other side of the world. Left behind her job, family and friends. And for what? So far, she had nothing. She'd enjoyed a lovely picnic with some strangers today, but what about tomorrow, and the day after that? She needed a plan. Resolute, she turned to march back down the mountain.

At the picnic area, Matilda removed her coat and sat on a bench. She'd worked up a sweat on the mountain and needed to cool off. The rest of the family had packed up while they were gone and had begun pulling out of the park, waving and honking goodbye as they went. She had to admit she'd had a nice time, enjoyed their company.

After they were gone, Rita was still packing things into the back of her truck. Matilda carried a folding chair and placed it in the bed. They both climbed into the truck, but Rita didn't start the engine. Instead, she leaned against the headrest with a sigh.

"So, what did you think of the clan?"

"I like them. They're friendly and welcoming. They made me feel right at home."

"I'm glad to hear it."

"No one knew anything about Tyler. At least, they weren't telling me if they did. I'm not sure what to do now. I guess I should go home."

"Is that what you want?"

"To go home? No, I don't want to, but I'm feeling a bit disappointed and lost. Also, a little crazy. Not sure why I even came."

Another sigh. "Don't leave yet. I have a confession to make. And don't get used to it, I'm not one to admit guilt. You may not see it happen ever again." She chuckled. "So, here's the truth ... Tyler Osbourne is my son."

Chapter Fourteen

Matilda gaped at Rita. "What?"

"He's my son. I didn't know who you were, why you were asking about him, so I kept quiet."

"I don't know what to say. I guess that makes sense." A sense of excitement at finally having something to hold onto, swept through Matilda. "So, can I ask where he is?"

"He's in the army, so he moves around. He's currently in Germany."

"Wow, I'm in shock. He's my first cousin, at least I think he is. According to my DNA profile. I really need to speak to him so I can find out."

"I know you believe he's your cousin, but I really don't think you've got the right Tyler," Rita said gently. "All of his cousins are accounted for. In my family, there's just me and my sister. I have Tyler and a daughter named Sophie. My sister, Helen, had one daughter, Julie. That's it. My husband didn't have any siblings. Tyler's father died a while back in a workplace accident, and my daughter, Sophie, lives in Colorado and she hasn't married or had children yet. So, it's not possible

Tyler has any relatives we don't know about. It must be another Tyler Osbourne."

Matilda's brow furrowed as she thought through the implications of what Rita was saying. It was another dead end.

"I'm sorry," Rita continued. "I know you were hoping for more than that. But I can assure you, he doesn't have any long lost first cousins. It isn't possible."

"That's okay. Thanks for letting me know." Matilda slumped in her seat.

They drove back to the bed and breakfast together. Matilda chatted about her family in Australia, her job working with animals. Rita talked about the cafe and how she'd inherited it from her father. The lake house and how much it meant to her. Matilda felt a connection with Rita. The woman was genuine, warm, had a big laugh and even bigger smile. There was something special about her that made Matilda want to get to know her better, spend time together.

"Do you have a boyfriend?" Rita asked.

"I did, back in Australia. Although he broke up with me before I came here. But he says he's just taking some time, so I'm not sure if it's a permanent break-up."

"How do you feel about him?"

Matilda leaned against the truck window, staring out into the gathering darkness. "I love him. I guess. I thought I did, anyway. We've been dating for two years. I kept waiting for him to pop the question. But then, we both got comfortable. We'd spend time together on the weekends, but our weekdays were our own. I didn't think much about him while I was working, or even after work when I was at home or out with friends, which I know is probably a bad sign. I honestly don't know how I feel about him anymore. When he broke up with me, I thought I'd be devastated. But those feelings never came."

Rita tutted. "It sounds to me like the break-up might have been the right thing to do."

"How can you tell? How did you know your husband was the one for you?"

Rita sighed, one hand on the steering wheel, the other resting on the gear stick. "We both just knew. I don't know how to describe it. We'd only been on three dates, and I was looking at this man across the table from me at the bowlin' alley. He was smiling about something, and he took a fry out of the basket and pushed it into his mouth, and I just knew. He was the man I would spend my life with. There wasn't a specific reason or anything like that. He felt like coming home, as though I'd known him forever. I was so comfortable around him, I didn't have to pretend to be anyone or wear a mask. It wasn't scary or intimidatin' to talk to him. We clicked. That was it."

"Wow. I wish I could say the same for me and Cam."

"I'd never felt anything like it before. Or since. It was special. We had a special kind of love, we always said that. And I miss him every day." Rita wiped her eyes.

"That must be hard. I hope I find love like that someday."

"You will, honey. But don't settle for less. Because let me tell you, even though we were so much in love, marriage was hard. We had a whole lotta ups and downs sometimes I thought we lived on a rollercoaster." She grinned. "You don't want to get on the marriage rollercoaster with a man you're not hopelessly in love with. You won't make it."

"What if I do love him?"

"You don't."

"How do you know?" Matilda asked, desperate for an answer that would make everything clear.

"Because when you're in love you know it. There's not a question anywhere in your soul. If you're doubtin', it's not love. Not the right kind that can make a marriage work, anyway."

After that, Matilda was quiet, watching the houses and shops they passed.

Rita dropped her off at the bed and breakfast, then waved goodbye. Matilda wandered up to the front door and let herself in. It was dark inside, which surprised her. There was a lit candle at the reception desk, but no one on duty.

A shiver ran through her. It was like walking into a haunted house. The old building creaked and groaned right then, making her jump. She was exhausted after a long day of socialising with strangers, standing in the cold, climbing a mountain. And now she had to face this darkened building alone? There was no one else around that she could see. And the only sound was some faint music in the distance, the wind in the eaves outside, and another creak of floorboards.

With a quick intake of breath, she headed for her room. If she could lock herself in there, she'd feel a lot more comfortable. When she reached the room, she found the door ajar. The whole situation was getting creepier by the moment. She pushed the door inwards, and poked her head through, heart in her throat.

"Hello?"

"Oh, hey," Ryan said.

He stood on a ladder, his tall frame casting a long shadow from a candle on the chest of drawers nearby.

"What's going on?"

"Sorry to disturb, the electricity is out and I'm giving everyone candles."

"I can see that. What's with the ladder?"

"I'm checking all the wiring. Trying to figure out what's going on. Something's tripped the electrical circuit. I'll have to get an electrician out tomorrow if the power hasn't come back on and I can't figure out what's causing the issues."

"Oh, okay. Well, do what you have to do. I'm glad you're here, actually. I thought no one was around, and it was a little spooky."

He smiled. "Should I tell you a scary story? You know, one of those campfire tales?"

"Don't you dare," she said, her nostrils flaring.

She marched into the bathroom to get ready for bed. When she emerged, he was still tinkering with the wiring. She sat on the sofa, curled her legs up beneath her with a gigantic yawn. As soon as he left, she would fall into bed. This jet lag was killing her. She couldn't manage to stay up until a decent bedtime yet. Although she'd done better today than she had the previous few.

"So are you some kind of electrician?" she asked.

He laughed. "Not exactly. I do a bit of this and that."

"You're the handyman."

"I guess you could call me that." He tested the blow heater she'd set up that morning. She'd found it in the closet and had needed a little extra heat to wake herself up.

"Rita, the woman who owns the Honeysuckle Cafe, told me you live next door to her at the lake?"

"That's right."

"Do you like it there?"

"It's good."

"Do you always use so many words?"

He looked at her, one eyebrow quirked. "No."

"Okay, great." Her fingers tapped out a rhythm on the arm of the sofa. "How long do you think this will take?"

"As long as it takes," he said absently, as he set aside the heater and moved onto the next appliance. "I'll be out of your hair soon enough."

"No hurry," she replied, with a yawn. She foraged around in her purse and found a Three Musketeers bar she'd bought at the corner store the previous day. She unwrapped it and took a bite. It wasn't the most nutritious dinner, but she couldn't bring herself to go out and find something better and they'd eaten a late lunch or maybe it was an early dinner at Stone Mountain. So really the candy bar was more like supper. Her bed was calling her name, and she looked at it longingly.

Then, her gaze shifted to Ryan. He was focused on what he was doing. Dressed in well-cut jeans and a grey sweater, he looked like the offspring of a construction worker and a GQ model. He wasn't her type. She'd always gone for the more bookish men with the earnest brow, who talked about classic literature and liked to rock climb on the weekends. But maybe her type was all wrong. None of them had ever given her the kind of feelings Rita had spoken of when she talked about falling in love with her husband. Would Matilda ever get to experience that kind of love? Probably not. She didn't have the right personality type for it. She was a serious kind of person, generally didn't let her emotions control her. Did people like Matilda ever really *fall* in love, or did they simply make a conscious choice to love someone and spend their lives together?

"Did you have a good day?" Ryan asked as he tested the mini fridge.

She yawned again, rested her head on the end of the sofa. "Yeah... I did. It was nice. Rita took me for a family picnic. I got to meet her lovely family, climbed Stone Mountain. It was fun."

"Rita's good people."

"But it's the wrong Tyler," she mumbled, her eyes drifting shut.

"Huh? What was that about Tyler? I didn't hear you."

"He's not the one." She tried to say more, but she was already asleep.

When she woke, she found herself being lifted by strong

arms from the sofa. He held her close where it was warm and she felt safe. She could stay in that place forever, it felt so good.

"Shhh, go back to sleep," she heard.

Then, he carried her nestled against his chest to the bed, set her down on the soft mattress, and pulled the covers up over her.

She didn't open her eyes, but she could feel him standing over her, watching. Then, he left. Her eyes blinked open briefly to see him blow out the candle and pull the door shut behind him. When he was gone, she fell immediately back into a deep slumber, unable to resist the pull of sleep any longer. And she dreamed of fried chicken, endless hiking through thick woods, and a tall, strong man ahead of her, always just out of reach.

Chapter Fifteen

TWENTY-SIX YEARS AGO

A year later, Helen had tried a dozen different pregnancy tests without any luck. Paul had visited three months ago, and they'd tried again for a baby. This time she was ready, excited, and couldn't wait to take the test. But it was negative. Again. At the rate they were going, they'd have their first child when she was ninety-five. They only saw each other twice a year, and clearly, she needed more time than that to get pregnant. It wasn't happening, and each negative test sent her into a spiral of self-doubt and despair. She'd begun to cling to the idea of having a baby as a way to help her out of the funk she was in.

The ward was quiet. She was on the night shift, and thankfully, there wasn't much going on. She often floated between wards and tonight was on duty at the oncology ward. The patients were asleep and everyone was stable. She strode through the hallways, careful not to let her shoes squeak on the tiles. The quiet sounds of the hospital ward at night comforted her. This was her happy place. Even though there was so much suffering all around her, she could do something to help. She had a concrete way to give to these people in a time when they needed it. She loved that about her job—it gave her a sense of purpose and meaning. Something she desperately needed in her life with Paul away.

Her flip-phone pinged. It was Rita.

> Hope you're having a good night. I'll come with you tomorrow if you like? Xo

Helen's stomach clenched. Tomorrow. The text reminded her of the appointment she had set up at the IVF clinic. She was excited about it but dreading it at the same time. It was like an admission of defeat.

> That would be great. I'll pick you up at eleven.

She returned to her desk and sat in front of the computer. Checking emails was a new ritual. But there was nothing of interest. She had a paper to read about the latest development in treatments for bed sores but couldn't seem to focus.

She lifted the kitchen phone off the wall and called Paul's base. He might not be available, but she'd try anyway. She was surprised when she heard was put through to his unit and he answered after only three rings, sounding sleepy.

"Hey sweetie," she said.

He yawned into the phone. "Baby, everything okay?"

"All good—I'm working but there's not much going on, so I thought I'd give you a call. How are you?"

"I'm okay. We had a rough few days so I'm trying to get some sleep."

"Sorry I woke you up."

"No, it's good. I want to hear your voice. I'll go right back to sleep after we hang up. I don't have any trouble doing that these days."

"I'm going to that IVF appointment tomorrow."

"Oh, that's right. Well, good luck, baby. I know you'll be fine. It's just information gathering, right?"

"That's right. We haven't committed to anything yet. But I'm still nervous. I don't know why I get so worked up about this stuff. I'm a nurse, I should be able to handle an appointment to talk about IVF."

"It's understandable," he said. "It's a big deal for us."

"Yeah, I don't know if I will even be able to get pregnant with help. And I hate to spend so much money if I'm unable to. It's a big risk." She pressed a hand to her face and groaned. "I really don't know what to do. I don't want to bankrupt us. We were saving for a house."

"We'll be fine. We'll figure it out somehow."

"Maybe I should just accept that I'm not going to have a baby. We could spend all our savings and still not have one. I don't know if we should do that."

"You've got to stop being so hard on yourself," he replied in a calm voice. "We're not going to make a perfect choice; we just have to make the choice we think is right. It might work out, it might not. But we've got to try, or we'll always regret it. We can make more money, but we can't go back and have a baby."

"You're right," she sighed. "Of course you're right. I'm so glad I have you to talk to. Even if you can't be here in person, it helps."

"I'm glad." He yawned. "Tell me something good."

"I've finished painting the living room. You would be so impressed with me. I have a streak of blue in my hair now and no idea how to get it out, but the room looks good. I think it does, anyway."

He laughed. "Blue hair, huh? Sounds sexy."

She grinned. "I'm glad you think so. It bodes well for my senior years."

"I wish I could be there to help you with that. You shouldn't be doing it all on your own."

"Don't worry, I got the low stink paint so I'm not dizzy at the end of the day. But it's still pretty bad. I think I'll see if I can stay at the lake house tomorrow night."

"That's a good idea. And hey, shoot me an email to let me know how it goes at your appointment."

"I will."

They told each other goodnight. She said how much she loved him. She always had to say it because she dreaded the thought of losing him without having said it before they hung up. The anxiety had gotten bad lately. Perhaps it was her worrying about getting pregnant, or the pressures of work, or the fact that he was in a war zone. Or maybe it was all of those things combined.

* * *

The next day, Helen picked up Rita from the lake house and they drove towards the city together in her four-door red sedan. Rita was unusually chatty, so Helen mostly listened. She always enjoyed her sister's company. They'd been close since Helen was born. Rita always said she'd been so delighted at having a younger sister that she'd taken over the responsibility of raising her. Their parents had watched with amusement as the five-year-old did her best to feed, bathe and dress Helen when she was big enough to manage it. They always said the two of them were inseparable, and nothing much had changed. Rita was the one person Helen relied upon.

"Do you think this is going to work?" she interjected suddenly.

Rita looked over at her. "What? The IVF?"

"Yeah."

"I think it will. Definitely. I'm sure there's nothing wrong, you just need a little help. And it's harder for you, having a husband out of the country all the time."

"Is it wrong? Should I wait until he's back? I mean... I don't know anyone who's done this. It seems so strange."

"He'll be back before you know it. He's only got two years left. You might not get pregnant for a little while, so maybe he'll be home in time for the birth. You never know. And it's worth giving this whole thing a try, what could go wrong?"

"That's true, I suppose."

"And I'm gonna be with you the whole time. Nothin' is happening today, we're only talking. That's it. You can listen, can't you?" Rita offered her a cheeky smile.

Helen's eyes narrowed. "Yes, I can listen."

"Great, that's all you need to do. We're not making any decisions or doing anything permanent. We're just talking and listening."

"Okay, I know you're right. I can do that."

"No need to worry. Just relax."

"I don't know if I can relax, but I'll try." Helen hadn't relaxed in months. Between work, worrying over her husband, exercising at the gym, volunteering at her church for fundraisers and prayer teams, and helping out her parents when they needed it, she hadn't spent much time on her own or doing anything relaxing. The only vacation time she'd had was when Paul visited, and she spent that time taking care of him and worrying about the day he had to leave.

"Maybe you should look into learning some relaxation techniques or somethin'?" Rita suggested.

"Do you know any?"

"I'm always relaxed. I don't need techniques." Rita chuckled.

"I can't believe you don't get stressed about the cafe. That place would give me a stomach ulcer."

Rita shrugged. "It's not so bad. It basically runs itself most of the time."

"You're always havin' some kind of emergency or crisis. Someone doesn't show up to work, something breaks down, the supplies don't arrive in time, or the fish is bad..."

"True, but I don't let it worry me too much. And I'm doing what I love, so I guess that helps."

"You really do love it, don't you?"

"That place is as much a part of me as you are." Rita sighed. "Although sometimes I wish it wasn't. It's a lot of work."

They arrived at the IVF clinic and waited side by side in the small, sterile room that jutted off the entry. There were children's toys in one corner, but no children playing with them. A television screen hung from the ceiling, playing a cartoon, but the sound was on mute. Instead, soft music filtered through speakers positioned about the space.

Rita leaned close to whisper. "You doing ok?"

Helen nodded. "I'm fine. I have to keep reminding myself what this is all for— I want a baby. I'm dying to have one. And this is the way to make that happen."

"Right. Hold onto that thought." Rita slid her hand into Helen's and squeezed.

They sat that way for a few minutes until the doctor called Helen in. She offered Rita a half smile and then followed the doctor into her office.

"I'm Dr. Arlington, won't you take a seat?"

"Hi, I'm Helen. Pleasure to meet you."

"You too, Helen. Let's get started."

They discussed her fertility, her goals, her health and everything else imaginable about her life. By the time they were done, Helen was exhausted, even though the appointment had only been for twenty minutes. She met Rita in the waiting room.

"Do you think you could drive? I'm done in."

"Sure, I'll drive." Rita wrapped an arm around Helen's shoulders and led her back to the car. "How'd it go?"

"I don't know. Fine, I guess. But she was real matter of fact about the whole thing. I've gotta have all these tests, and then they'll determine if I'm infertile. And after that we can decide what we want to do."

"Infertile?"

"Yeah, it sounded serious. Since we've been trying for a while, although, of course, not really since Paul has been gone. But she thinks there could be an issue and gave me all these pamphlets about IVF treatments, what to expect and all. It's a lot to take in. And I'm stressed out about the whole thing." She climbed into the car, then leaned back against the headrest. "I don't know what to do. I'm so anxious, tired, overworked ... and now this on top of it. It might be the straw that breaks the camel's back."

Rita started the car engine. It was afternoon, and traffic was already backing up for the peak hour rush. She pulled into the nearest lane. "I think you should take one step at a time. You don't have to do it all at once. Or even think about it all. What's the next step?"

"I have to get a blood test done."

"Great, you can do that. It's not so hard. Just one step. Then, when you've done that, think about the next step. You're letting yourself get overwhelmed because you're focusin' on the whole, big thing. That would be too much for anyone to manage."

"Thanks, Rita. You always know what to say."

"I try," she replied. "I hope you know how much I love you."

Helen smiled at her. "I love you too, sis. You're the best. I couldn't do this without you."

"Paul loves you as well, and I know he wishes he could be here. He's a good man."

"True..." Helen replied with a sigh. "I wish he was here."

"You know what we should do?" Rita asked as they sat, still waiting for the traffic to move.

"What's that?"

"We should go dancing!"

"What? Dancin'? I don't know..."

"We should put on some skimpy dresses, overdo our makeup, and hit the town. We haven't done that in ages, and I bet your anxiety could be solved by a night out. You need to have some fun. You're young. You shouldn't be living like a sixty-year-old woman. All you do is work, chores, help out with Mom and Dad, and go to appointments. You need to let loose and enjoy your life. Besides, you might be pregnant before too much longer, if all goes well. Now is your chance to live a little. Jimmy will watch the kids. We can buy something to eat while we're out. It'll be fun."

"You make some good points." Helen smiled. "Okay, let's go dancing."

Chapter Sixteen

CURRENT DAY

Matilda's phone rang and woke her up. It took her a minute to realise what the sound was since she was dead to the world. It was early. Too early to be getting out of bed. Still dark outside. She slapped one hand around on the bedside table until she found the phone, then held it to her ear, eyes still squeezed shut.

"Hello?" Her voice was gravelly, she cleared her throat.

"Is that you, Tilly? You sound different. What's wrong?" Cam's nasal voice boomed down the line at her, startling her into wakefulness.

"Huh? Oh, I'm jet lagged. That's all. I'm fine. I was sleeping. You know there's a fourteen hour time difference, right?"

"I forgot about that. Besides, I can't seem to work out when is the best time to call you, but I figure you'll be happy to hear from me at any time. Right?"

She sat up and rubbed the sleep from her eyes. "Uh ... yeah. Of course. What's going on, Cam?"

"I miss you. When are you coming home?"

She frowned. "You miss me? You broke up with me."

"We both decided we should take some time to think about our relationship, where we're headed. And I've done that. Have you?"

What was this? Some kind of retrograde amnesia? Or was he gaslighting her?

"Okay, I'm glad you've been thinking about us. I have too." She hadn't much. Had been too busy enjoying her vacation to pay him much mind. But she'd given him a few moments of thought when she was talking to Rita about him.

She pushed the covers off, remembering in that instant how she'd wound up there. She'd been carried to her bed and gently placed beneath the covers. Ryan had even pulled the covers up high under her chin and tucked her in. She recalled it all with vivid clarity, and it made her skin tingle.

"Hello? Are you listening to me?" Cam sounded annoyed.

Matilda tried to focus. She padded over to the coffee maker on top of the set of drawers against the wall and pressed the on button. It immediately began percolating coffee.

"Hmmm? What's that? Sorry, I missed what you were saying."

"I asked when you're coming home? My boss and his wife are coming over to my place for dinner in two weeks and I need you here."

She searched one of the drawers for a clean mug, found it and set it on top of the drawers. "Huh? You need me to be at a meeting? I'm sorry, Cam, I'm in America. You know that."

He grunted. "I know, Captain Obvious. I'm asking you to come home so you can help me out."

"You want me to host a dinner for your boss ... at your house?" She'd done it a dozen times before. It was no big deal. But they'd been dating at the time. And even though she thought it a little strange for him to ask her to do that since they didn't live together and weren't married, she'd given in because that's what she always did. She hated to cause any conflict. But this time was different. "We broke up, Cam."

He huffed. "I already told you, it wasn't a break-up. How many times do you need me to repeat myself? I need you here. I miss you. When are you coming back? You're not even having a vacation. I don't know what you're still doing there."

"I'm looking for my family. Which I told you about before I left. Why are you so invested in me being at this meeting?" She poured the coffee into the mug, using her shoulder to hold her phone in place against her ear.

"You know how my company is. They like partners to be stable, settled, married. It's just how they operate. It's anti-quated, but it is what it is. I can't change it. At least not yet anyway. We'll see how I do in a few years time."

"But we're not married, Cam."

"I realise that, Matilda, but..."

She hesitated. "Look, I've got to go. I've got a big day ahead of me and someone woke me up before the crack of dawn. So I might as well take a walk before breakfast. Unless there's something else you need..."

His silence spoke volumes. He was angry. She could tell. It almost crackled down the phone line. But for some strange reason, she didn't really much care. She hadn't ever noticed before just how whiny and entitled he could be, and she suddenly found it highly unattractive.

"So, you're not coming?" he snapped.

She pressed a smile to her face. His true colours always showed with the slightest pressure applied. "No, I'm not coming. We broke up. You may want to pretend otherwise, but we're no longer a couple and that was your choice. I suggest you find someone else to play house with for your boss."

She pressed the button to end the call, suddenly nostalgic for the old-fashioned phone that could be slammed down to

111

hang up. Never mind, no doubt he got the picture. Her smile grew until she felt it in the depths of her soul. She'd stood up to him. Finally. It was over. And all she felt was happiness and relief.

Matilda dressed warmly, then headed out. By now, the sun had tinged the eastern sky with yellow and orange. Her breath billowed like a cloud of smoke in front of her face as she stepped into the cold morning. She pulled on gloves and slapped her hands together, then shoved them into her coat pockets.

Which direction should she take? To the left was the small town of Covington, but it was a long walk in that direction. More of a drive really, probably close to half an hour by car. She was quite far out in the country, and she wasn't sure what was in the other direction. She turned to the right and started out along the side of the road. There was no sidewalk, something she'd noticed during her time in Atlanta. Very few people walked anywhere, and there was no path designated for walking either. But she loved to take walks, they helped her think clearly and gave her a sense of peace and joy. They were an important ritual each day.

She walked for a good fifteen minutes before she spotted the glimmering surface of the lake through the bare branches of some oak trees. A sign on the side of the road read *Jackson Lake*. This was the lake Rita lived on. Her house must be nearby.

Matilda took the turn down towards the lake. She'd only seen the occasional car on the way here, but now the road was quiet. It dipped and curved downward. Beside the lake, she walked past a row of houses. Most were older, some in dire need of love, but a few were modern and spacious, gleaming in the morning sunlight.

The only greenery was a few firs, and birds flitted between the bare tree branches. The sun was moving up the sky, warming her up, and she unzipped her jacket. Matilda puffed lightly from climbing a gentle hill, then spotted a mailbox with *Osbourne* printed on the side. This must be Rita's house. It was a single-story bungalow painted in dark maroon and browns. Surrounded by shrubbery, it looked cozy and comfortable. There were gnomes and bird statues in the garden. One gnome lay on its side next to an upside-down rowing boat. Behind the house was a footpath that led to a dock, jutting out over the edge of the shimmering water. And an old boat sat idle, moving gently on the wake of a passing pontoon.

She looked to the left—that must be Ryan's house. It looked to be around the same vintage as Rita's house, but it was in the throes of renovation. There was scaffolding around the upper level. A new deck had been added, the timber still fresh and bright. The yard was piled with timber and other building supplies. The dock on his property was old, mouldy and in need of repair.

Just then, Ryan stepped outside, shirtless and holding a giant mug in one hand. His sweatpants were slung low around his hips. His entire body was toned and tanned. His breath puffed in a white cloud in front of him and he looked up at the sky, then stood, surveying the lake for a few moments. Sipped his coffee and then stepped back inside.

Matilda realised she was staring. How mortifying it would've been if he'd turned to see her standing still, clearly looking directly at him and his property. She'd frozen in place. Didn't want to catch his eye. She quickly spun on her heel to return to the bed and breakfast, her heart racing. That was a close call.

Chapter Seventeen

TWENTY-FIVE YEARS AGO

With a shiver, Helen wrapped the belt of her cardigan around her waist, hugged herself. It was snowing. It hardly ever snowed in Atlanta, but it was today. There was a thin white blanket covering the grassy area by the road. It wasn't sticking on the dock or the lake yet, but it had left a few flakes behind on the fir trees on the hill.

She wiped her nose with a tissue, then sneezed. She had an awful cold. It had come on strong two days earlier with the temperature drop. And Helen was ready for it to be over.

"Are you coming?" she called.

Rita appeared at the door. "Hold your horses."

"Time is of the essence," Helen countered with a smirk.

"Rome wasn't built in a day." Rita slid her feet into a pair of boots.

"Let's get this party started!"

"Patience is a virtue," Rita crooned.

Helen laughed. "Okay, I'm out. I can't think of any others."

"So … I win?"

Helen hated to lose. She huffed. "Fine, yes, you win."

"Where are we going?"

"I need to get a few things at the store. Pregnancy test, of course."

"That's right, you had another implantation a few weeks ago, didn't you?"

Helen swallowed, her stomach churning. Another implantation of embryos. Another disappointment incoming. It was six months since she'd first stepped into that IVF clinic and since then she'd gone through a battery of tests, treatments, egg harvesting, hormones and now implantations. It'd been the hardest six months of her life. Her moods had swung up and down, Paul was out of reach most of the time on various missions, and she'd been doing a lot of night shifts for some reason. She'd scheduled a time to speak with her supervisor about that, although she wasn't sure it'd make much difference. Lack of sleep really knocked her around.

"Cathy called earlier," Rita said, with an eye roll.

The two sisters walked to Helen's car.

"Really? What did the ice queen want?"

"She's upset that Tyler got a slot at the daycare over on Fairview Street. We've been on the waiting list for two years. He finally got Thursdays and Fridays. And apparently, she wanted that slot for her precious Brent."

"So? There's nothing you can do about it. The daycare chooses who gets those spots."

"I know, but she wanted me to give it to her. Said she needed it more than me since I only work at the cafe." Rita snorted. "Some cousin she is. Who needs enemies with family like her around?"

"She never thinks of anyone else's needs. You can't take the kids to the cafe with you all the time. It's not safe, for one thing."

"And they get so bored. I try to keep them close by, but Tyler can only colour for so long before he starts playing up. And I have to call Mom to come and get them."

"Just ignore her. She's always trying to cause trouble." Helen started the car. "We should grab some Chick-Fil-A on the way. I'm starving."

"Sounds good. I could eat a chicken sandwich and waffle fries."

"I'm going to get a chicken biscuit. I've been craving them lately."

They stopped at the restaurant's drive through and placed their order, and then ate on their way to Walmart where Helen picked out a pregnancy test.

"Should I use the bathroom here or go home?" she asked, waving the test in front of Rita.

Rita shrugged. "Do it here if you like. I don't mind waiting. Also, I need to get a few things for the cafe."

Helen wandered through the massive store in search of the bathroom. Finally, she found it in the back. She carried the stick back out with her to the sink and washed her hands, then stared at her reflection in the mirror. She looked tired. There were dark smudges beneath her eyes, and a few wrinkles on their edges she hadn't noticed before. The idea of taking a nap sounded really good. She could go to sleep right there on the counter if she laid her head down.

She peeped at the test. There was a pink line. The same pink line she always saw. Never mind. She'd just have to do another implantation. Although every time she did the procedure, it cost them money. A lot of money. They wouldn't be able to afford many more. But she was okay with that. She'd come to terms with the possibility of them never having a baby. There was nothing more she could do about it—she'd done everything right, followed every piece of advice from the doctor. And she would have to be okay with their life looking a little different to what they'd planned. She didn't have a choice. But how would Paul feel about it?

With the pregnancy test in hand, she traipsed back to where Rita waited, chewing on a red vine, the rest of the bag poking out of her jacket pocket.

"Want one?"

"Thanks." Helen took the red vine and bit into it. She handed the pregnancy test to her sister.

"What's it say?"

"Not pregnant. Again."

"Are you sure?" Rita held it up and studied the test closely. Her eyes narrowed. "I swear that's a second pink line."

"What? No... I didn't see anything."

"There," she said, pointing.

Helen looked. "It's so faint though."

"It doesn't matter if it's faint. That's a second line. Mine looked like this when I had Sophie."

Helen's eyes widened. "Are you serious?"

Rita grinned. "You're pregnant, hon."

Emotion flooded through Helen. Her vision blurred. She sobbed. "I'm pregnant!"

"You're pregnant!"

She jumped up and down in place, then leapt at her sister for a hug. They danced around in a circle together, both squealing with delight. Finally, they made their way back out to the car. They chattered in excitement together all the way back to the lake house, their shopping errands completely forgotten. Helen wanted to tell her parents the good news, and to call her husband in private. It'd been hard to reach him lately, but she'd give it a try anyway. He'd be so excited.

"You're not going to tell everyone, though, are you?" Rita asked as they pulled into the driveway.

"Why not?"

"Usually people wait until after the first trimester to make it public. You know ... just in case."

She hadn't thought about that. What if it went wrong? What if she lost the baby? Her excitement waned a little at that prospect.

"I'm sure it will all be fine," added Rita hastily. "Don't worry about that. You're going to be great, and the baby is going to have such wonderful, loving parents. I can't wait to see you raising her or him."

Helen looked at her sister. She loved Rita more than she could say. Always ready with encouragement. Always building her up. "Thanks. You're the best."

Inside, they found their parents having a cup of coffee. They were arguing over a scrabble match.

"Onsen is not a word," Dad hissed, shaking his head.

Mum set her hands on her hips. "Yes it is. It's Japanese."

"We're not in Japan, are we? We're in the good old United States of America. And in this country, we speak English."

"It's still a word."

"You can't use foreign jibber-jabber in scrabble. You're breaking all the rules."

"I don't think that's a rule," Mum said, reaching for the box to read over the instructions.

Dad threw his hands up in the air with a groan. "I give up. Use whatever combination of letters you like. You're always right."

They bickered more these days since Dad wasn't working at the cafe any longer, but they always made up. Helen cleared her throat and held out her hands to calm them. "Hello? Can you two stop fighting over Scrabble for a moment, please?"

Mom and Dad both fell quiet and looked up at her. Mom smiled warmly. Dad scowled.

"What is it, honey?"

"I'm pregnant!" She declared proudly.

They all celebrated then. Mom brought out the Hawaiian punch with ice cubes and slices of lime. Dad found the chocolate cake Mom had made the day before and cut slices for everyone. And they all sat together around the kitchen table and talked about the fun times ahead with another baby in the family.

"I want to see if I can reach Paul. I'm dying to tell him." Helen stood and excused herself, grabbed the phone from the kitchen, then hurried out to the sunroom to be alone.

She dialled and waited while it rang and then was transferred, her heart pounding.

He answered quickly and his voice was clear. "Hey, honey."

Tears clogged her throat. "Hey. You're back at base?"

"Yeah, we got in last night. I slept like a log. I was so tired. How are you?"

"I'm good. I have news."

"Good news, I hope?"

She smiled widely, her eyes filling with tears. "I'm pregnant."

"You're pregnant? That's fantastic. I'm so happy."

"Me too. I wish you were here."

"I wish I could give you a big hug. But I'm thinking of it, and I'll definitely give you one the moment I get back stateside. I promise. Wow. This is so great. It'll help keep me going. I've been struggling ... well, anyway, you don't need to hear about all that. You should take care of yourself. Get some rest."

"I'll try. I've got to do something about these night shifts."

"Yeah, talk to your boss. I'm sure they can do something for you, especially now there's a baby on the way."

There was a loud explosion in the background. Helen hesitated. "Paul?"

"I've got to go, honey. We've got incoming mortar fire."

"Take care of yourself. Get under cover," she shouted, over the noise of more and bigger explosions.

"I will. I love you."

"I love you so much," she replied, her voice thick with tears.

The phone line went silent. Helen stared at it, weeping. Tears fell down her cheeks and wet her shirt. The sobs welled up inside her, making her whole body shake. This was unfair. He shouldn't be so far away, in danger. Not while she was carrying their baby inside of her. Something primal within her wanted to scream, to rage, to go to him and drag him home to safety. But she couldn't do that. She had to hold it together, be the supportive wife.

He was struggling, she'd heard his admission and knew him well enough to know he was holding back and not telling her all of it. She'd worried about him for months. He'd seemed down, not himself. And now he had something more to live for, she hoped it would give him the strength to pull through these final months away.

She made her way out to the kitchen, wiping her eyes as she went. She plastered a smile onto her face and the family all gaped at her.

"What's wrong, honey?" Mom asked, rushing to her side.

"I don't know ... there were explosions. What if he's hurt?"

Dad and Rita joined them, and they all locked together in an embrace with Helen at their centre.

"It'll be okay. I know it will," Rita said, her voice thin.

"Sure, he's a smart man, he'll find a place to shelter," added Dad.

But his eyes were dull, and her heart felt hollow.

"I can't live without him," Helen said with a sob.

Mom squeezed her shoulder. They all stood in the kitchen, in silence, heads bowed, filled with worry.

Chapter Eighteen

The walk to The Honeysuckle Cafe was about an hour and there were no footpaths, so Matilda caught an Uber there. Set in the heart of Covington, the place was clearly an institution. Locals thronged to buy coffee, pastries, burgers and fries, or to sit in the vine-covered enclosed patio to eat a meal.

The cafe was almost full, but Matilda managed to find a single table where she could sit. She set up her laptop and pulled up the US immigration website while a young woman with a guitar sang folk songs quietly in the background. She was mining for information on visas. Surely, she could find some way to stay in the country. She had six months on her current visa but couldn't work. And she'd have to find some kind of job if she was going to stay much longer, or she'd use up all her savings and put herself in a bind.

"Matilda, honey! It's good to see you again. Can I get you something?" Rita was dressed in a cornflower blue apron over a white shirt and jeans. She had a cornflower blue ribbon tied up in her hair, and the colour matched her eyes perfectly.

"I'd love a burger with fries and a cherry coke please."

"Coming right up. And I'll join you. I haven't eaten a thing all day."

After her order was ready, Rita sat at the table and ate a chicken caesar salad while Matilda enjoyed her delicious hamburger.

"I don't know what sauce you use on these, but I can't get enough," she said around a mouthful.

Rita nodded. "Family secret."

Matilda liked the idea of a family's secret recipe, especially when she might be part of that family. But was she? No matter what Rita said, Matilda couldn't shake the feeling that she was connected to this family. The more time that passed, the harder it was to deny. It felt strange to have such an intimate tie to someone she barely knew. But it also felt good. She could see the similarities between herself and Rita the more she got to know her. They shared mannerisms, a nose and even had the same posture. Likely, Rita's hair had been blonde when she was younger, now it was a sandy grey colour. And her eyes were blue, just like Matilda's. Rita might deny it, but they were related. She was sure of it.

"What are you working on?" Rita asked.

Matilda had put the laptop away in her bag. She waved a hand towards it. "Oh, I was looking up immigration visas. I thought I might try to find some work so I don't empty my bank account while I'm here."

"How long will you stay?"

"I don't know. I'd like to get to know you and the rest of the family a little bit. I really do think there's a connection between us. I know you aren't sure about it, but it's got to be you. You're Tyler's mother. And I can see a family resemblance. Don't you think?"

"You may be right about that, honey."

"So, I thought I might stay for a while, see how I go. But I need to be able to make some money." She felt shy, vulnerable opening up that way.

"I'm so glad you're stayin'. I'd love to spend more time together. Lord knows, I'm not likely to ever fly all the way to Australia." She cackled loudly. "That flight is far too long for these old bones. And I've never left the country before."

Matilda couldn't argue with that. The flight had been awful, and she was dreading the return trip. "I don't blame you. It's about twenty-four hours of travel. It wreaks havoc on your REM cycle."

"I'll bet it does. I might have a solution for you, though. Why don't you work here at the cafe? We're always looking for waiters and kitchen staff. You could help me out and I could pay you. It's a win, win."

"Really? Wow, that would be amazing. Although, I don't have a work visa yet."

"Oh pish, we can figure that-all out. In the meantime, I'll bet you could get a social security card over at the office across town. They're not real picky about the details. And I can pay you in cash, you just report that income when you're set up with your number."

"That would work. Thank you so much, Rita. I really appreciate it. And I'll have to find a place to stay as well. The Bed and Breakfast is too expensive long term."

"You can stay with me, honey. That's if you don't mind being in close quarters. I don't want to make you feel as though you have to say yes. It's up to you, and I won't be offended if you'd rather not."

"I would love that. It would be a godsend. You have no idea. Wow, thank you again. I'll pay rent."

"Never mind. We can figure those details once you're all moved in. Maybe you can help me keep the place going. I haven't been up to doing much physical labor lately."

"I'm happy to help in any way I can."

"Good, it's settled."

They ate in silence for a few moments, but Matilda had been dying to ask about the rest of the family. She still didn't quite know how she fit in, but she wanted to find out all about each of them. Who were they? What did they do? Where was she connected? All she knew was that Rita's son was her cousin, which meant that Rita was her aunt. But how that was possible, they still hadn't figured out.

"Can you tell me about your sister?"

Rita hesitated. "She died a while back. Her heart."

"I'm so sorry to hear that." Matilda's stomach fell.

"She had a rough trot for a while there. But I'm hoping you'll get a chance to meet Julie, her daughter. She's away at college right now in Athens. Attends the University of Georgia. Gooooo Dawgs!" Rita's eyes lit up, and she shouted the last two words.

"Sic 'em. Woof, woof!" The crowd in the cafe erupted in response, their chant in unison.

Rita chuckled, and Matilda gazed around in awe, enjoying the spontaneous camaraderie of the locals.

"What was that?" she asked, laughing.

"The Bulldogs are the college football team. We take our college football seriously 'round here."

Matilda shook her head. "Wow, I love that. I can't wait to meet Julie. And what about Tyler and Sophie?"

"As I said, Tyler's in the army. Last I spoke to him, he was in Germany. But he's due back stateside in a couple of months. If you're still around, you might could meet him then. Sophie's busy in Colorado. She doesn't get back here real often."

"I'm looking forward to meeting Tyler."

"He won't know anything, mind you."

"What do you mean?"

"About your connection. He won't be able to answer any

questions, because he doesn't know. I'm still not sure why he loaded his DNA onto that website. But I'm sure he had his reasons."

"Who *would* know? I need to find out how I'm connected to your family."

"I would be the most likely person to know how that works. And I ain't got a clue." She scratched her head. "That's the darnedest thing I ever heard. And I'm still in shock over it."

"I'm with you on that one," Matilda replied. "But I'm glad we can be in shock together. At least I'm not alone in it any longer."

Chapter Nineteen

The next morning, Matilda woke early again. She was feeling better than she had been. Her jet lag was under control, although she still couldn't manage to sleep in. Which worked out fine for her, since she'd always been a morning person and loved to go for a run to start each day.

She set off around seven o'clock, as soon as it was light enough. It was another overcast day, and the air was chilly. She dressed warmly in a puffer jacket and wound a scarf around her neck, then jogged in the direction of the lake. She'd planned to meet Rita, to walk through the house and get a key. She would move in that afternoon. And she couldn't be more excited. It finally seemed as though things were working out for her, and she was looking forward to spending more time with Rita.

She hadn't called Stella to update her on what she'd discovered yet. She was anxious about what Stella would say. No one would ever replace her family, but now she had another family. Would Stella be jealous? She wasn't sure how her sister would take it. Especially the part about her staying longer, living with Rita, and working at the cafe. She'd have to tell her family about these developments soon, but maybe she could put it off for another day.

When she reached the lake, she could see the steam rising from the water's surface and mingling with the fog that hung around the lowlands. As she ran by, a group of ducks quacked and wagged their tails, heads bobbing.

She ran around the edge of the lake counterclockwise, then turned to head back. It was a lot bigger than she'd realised, and the shoreline bobbed, curved, circled and wove its way through thickets of trees and bushes. Just when she thought it would turn one way, it went the other. There was no way she could jog around the entire thing.

On the way back towards Rita's house, she saw Ryan. He was working on his house, a tool belt slung low around his hips. He wore a half-buttoned, bone-coloured jacket, over a pair of jeans, and a knit hat on his head. He looked like he'd just finished shooting a construction commercial.

"Good morning," she said, formally.

He glanced up, smiled. "Hey there, Aussie. Whatcha doing out in this cold weather?"

She stopped running, stood panting with her hands on her thighs. "I thought that was pretty obvious."

"You visiting Rita?"

She nodded. Straightened. "She's offered to let me stay with her."

"Well, that's nice of her." He frowned. "You staying long?"

"I'm not sure how long I'll be here. It turns out that she's my aunt."

"Your aunt? How's that work?"

"I have no idea." She laughed.

He grinned. "Okay then. I guess ... welcome to the neighbourhood."

"Thanks. She's also offered to let me work at her cafe,

although I haven't got a visa yet. I've been looking into it, but I'm not sure I can get one. She thinks it'll be easy. But I don't know ... working at a cafe isn't exactly a high-level and in-demand skill for an immigrant visa."

"Yeah ... sounds tricky."

"And I'll run out of money if I don't get some work soon."

"What do you usually do for money?"

"I'm a vet," she replied. "I suppose I could try to do that here, but it's more of a long-term type of job. And once again, I don't have a visa."

"I hope it works out," he replied. "I've got to get to work myself. See you around."

"Yeah, I'm sure I'll run into you, neighbour."

He gave her a mock salute and sauntered off towards his truck while Matilda set off in a jog to the house next door. She stopped at the entryway and looked around. The lake was so beautiful and peaceful. It was quiet but for the sound of the occasional duck and the gentle lapping of the water at the dock. Drawing in a deep breath, she knocked on the door.

Rita opened it and gave her a big hug that squeezed the breath right back out of her lungs. She laughed, stumbling forwards. A large black dog greeted her with a tail wag and half-hearted bark.

"You're home!" Rita declared. "Come on in, honey. I'll show you around the place. Here is your key. And don't mind Blue, he don't bite."

"Wow, thanks. This house is so nice. It's got a really peaceful feel to it."

"I love it. My parents raised me and my sister here, and then gave it to me. So, I've lived in one place my whole life."

"That's so nice. My parents' house in Kingscliff is a little like that. I haven't lived there since I left home at eighteen to go to university. But we always go back there for holidays. I guess we'll have to sell it now that Dad's gone."

"Maybe you could keep it?" Rita said, stopping in the kitchen.

"Yeah, maybe."

"Here's the kitchen. Feel free to help yourself to anything —food, drinks, whatever you need. It's all here. I'm not great at keeping the fridge and pantry stocked, but if it's here, you're welcome to it."

"Okay, great. Thanks."

"Now, come with me." She led Matilda down a dark hallway. "Those are the kids' rooms. They don't use them anymore, of course. But if they come to stay, they like to be in their room. And this used to be their playroom, now it's a den and an office. Your room is here." She opened a door and waved Matilda inside.

A queen-sized bed sat in the centre of the room flanked by chests of drawers. There was a television set perched on one of them. The furniture was old style, Matilda guessed it was from the nineteen eighties. But it was all in good shape and made from hardwood that was clean and polished. The bed was made up with a floral comforter and a bouquet of floral pillows and cushions. The entire room smelled of lavender.

"This is beautiful. Thank you."

"You've got a bathroom here, and a walk in closet."

"Perfect."

"Make yourself at home and welcome to my lake house."

Chapter Twenty

The following Sunday, Rita decided to throw a party to welcome Matilda to the family. That morning, Matilda attended an enormous Baptist church with Rita. There were thousands sitting in the pews. It took them half an hour in a traffic jam to get in and out of the parking lot. The service was lovely if somewhat different to what she was accustomed to. Everyone was dressed formally in their Sunday best, and the pastor wore makeup while a camera crew filmed him preaching. The music was well done, and there was a small stage drama involving some very cute children, which she enjoyed. Nothing like the much smaller casual services with electric guitar-led music and a pastor wearing shorts she'd been part of in Brisbane.

After church, they hurried home and got everything set up. There were trestle tables lined up against the walls of the living room and kitchen. Matilda covered them with white tablecloths. She set up a punch bowl along with a bucket full of ice into which she thrust various soda bottles—or Coke, as Rita called them, regardless of their flavour—and a huge vat of sweet tea with enough sugar to propel them each directly into a diabetic coma.

Soon, family members began to arrive and casserole dishes were added to the trestle tables. There were casseroles of every kind—green bean, hash brown, carrot soufflé, sweet potato soufflé, ambrosia along with rotisserie chicken, sliced ham, turkey and chicken wings. Dessert was piled onto a single table in the kitchen, and Matilda eyed off her favourite pies—including pumpkin, pecan and key lime. There was also Cool Whip to go with every dessert.

The same crowd came as she'd met at Stone Mountain, and now she was beginning to learn some of their names. There was Cathy, a middle-aged woman with a bouffant and bright blue eyeshadow. Earl, who looked to be about ninety-five, had a silent laugh that accompanied his body shaking. He laughed a lot. And there were a dozen children who darted in and out amongst the adults, grabbing handfuls of food as they went and squealing at a high decibel level.

Matilda had never been around such a large and vocal family, and she really liked it. Such a contrast to her quiet and serious family gatherings back at home. Her Brisbane family were studious and high-achieving, and unlikely to go on an adventure with her. This Covington family seemed to be curious and extroverted. A lot more like she was. She felt at home there. Even if it was all still strange and new.

She lined up with the rest of the group to fill her plate with goodies, then found a seat against a wall by the piano to eat. Rita was busy filling glasses with tea and chatting with family members. But soon, Cathy came to sit by Matilda. She lowered herself into a chair with a sigh and set her tea down beneath the chair.

"Now, don't y'all knock that over."

"I wouldn't dream of it," Matilda replied. "How's things, Cathy?"

Cathy fixed her with a piercing stare. "You're still here?"

Matilda hesitated. "Yep, still here."

"Why are you here, again? I can't recall what Rita said about you."

Rita overheard and came to join them. "Oh, hi Cathy, I see you've met Matilda. She's from Australia and thinks she has some kind of family connection to us. From a DNA test. Remember? I told you about that?"

Cathy frowned. "DNA? I don't know about that. How does that work?"

"Well, Tyler is my cousin, but we're still trying to figure out how."

"Or if it's even right. I've still got my doubts," Rita added. "Some kind of mix up, most likely. Although I can't shake the feeling that you're family. You look the spitting image of Helen, my sister. Did I tell you that?"

Matilda shook her head as she swallowed a bite of turkey. "No, you didn't."

"Well, you favour her a little, that's true," Cathy added, "although I wouldn't say spitting image."

"How are you two related?" Matilda asked.

Cathy and Rita exchanged a look.

Cathy seemed irritated. "We're cousins. My daddy and hers were brothers. Course, they're both gone now, so there's not much holding us together these days. Except the café, of course."

Matilda shot Rita a questioning look. Rita forced a smile. "Oh now, let's not get into all of that today, Cathy. Matilda's our guest. She doesn't need all the dirty laundry on day one."

"She'd best know what she's getting into, if you ask me." Cathy shook her head. "You can't trust this one." She pointed a dinner roll at Rita.

Matilda didn't ask. She could see by the look of anger on Rita's face that it was better to leave it alone. Although she was more curious than she could say. What had driven a wedge between these two cousins? Something involving the cafe?"

"Well, I never..." Rita's face went pale. She clutched Matilda's arm so tight it hurt.

"Rita?" Matilda reached for her, but it was too late.

Rita crumpled to the floor in a pile. Matilda jumped up with a shout. "Someone call 911!"

She bent over Rita, who patted her hand. "No, no ... there's no need for an ambulance. I just felt a little faint is all. I'll be okay in a moment."

"You look pale," Matilda said as she squeezed Rita's shoulder. "We'll get you checked out in case. Okay?"

Rita lay back on the floor with a sigh. "Okay. That'll be fine."

* * *

In the end, the paramedics wanted to take Rita with them to the hospital. They wouldn't let Matilda ride with her, but Julie had been called by someone in the group and was on her way from Athens to meet them at Piedmont Hospital. Matilda watched them leave, worry eating at her.

"She'll be just fine," someone said, then patted Matilda on the shoulder.

Soon, everything was packed up and cleaned up and the entire group had gone home. Matilda was left by herself in the quiet lake house. She'd never felt so alone.

The house phone rang, and she rushed to answer it.

"Hello?"

"Hey there, sugar, it's Rita. I thought I'd give you an update."

She exhaled with relief. "Rita, I was so worried."

"Oh ,you're sweet to worry. But I'm here at the hospital. Already comfortable in a room since they've decided to keep me overnight. Julie is here, and she's making sure everyone is taking good care of me. Are you okay?"

It was just like Rita to be concerned about her when she was the one in hospital. Matilda squeezed her eyes shut. "I'm fine. Everyone went home a while ago. They did a great job of cleaning up so there's not much for me to do."

"Well, that's good. They're a wonderful bunch."

"Did they figure out what's wrong with you?"

"Something to do with my heart, but nothing for you to fret over. It's a little temperamental is all, and gives me trouble now and then. It'll be all right."

"Just as long as you're okay."

"I'm fine, sugar. Just fine. I'll see you tomorrow."

"Okay, get some sleep."

"I will."

When she hung up the phone, Matilda stared at the wall, processing what she'd just heard. It was her heart — that seemed like something they all should be worried about. Was she downplaying it? Or was it really no big deal? There was no way for her to know. But maybe Julie would fill in the details when they met. It was frustrating not having a car, since it was a long drive to the hospital. And even if she decided to take Rita's truck, which Rita had assured her was fine, she'd have to drive on the other side of the road. She wasn't sure she was ready for that yet.

Outside, she stood looking at Rita's truck, keys in hand. Maybe she could do it. The truck was an older model and had a gear stick. The shifter was also on the other side, she'd have to change gears with her right hand. Not that she'd ever learned how to drive stick. Stick is what Rita called it, rather than manual. She thought the description was apt.

"You thinking of stealing that truck?" Ryan's voice was teasing.

She turned to see him walking up his driveway from the mailbox, letters in hand.

With a frown on her face, she inhaled a deep breath. "I'm thinking of driving it. Although I don't know how to drive stick, and I've never driven on the right side of the road."

"Okay. Is there something you need in particular?"

"Rita is in hospital, and I thought I should visit her — it's probably too late tonight, but maybe tomorrow."

"She's in hospital?" He blanched. "What happened?"

"Something to do with her heart. She assures me she's okay, but I'm worried about her."

"I can drive, if you like."

"Really? I don't want to be any trouble."

"I don't mind. I'd like to see she's okay myself. Do you want to learn how to drive, or have me drive you there?"

"Maybe both?" She hesitated. What was she getting herself into? He was arrogant, rude, clearly didn't like her. And she would be stuck in a car with him for at least an hour if he drove her to the hospital. Driving lessons would mean them spending even more time together.

"I'll let you drive around the lake, then we can head to the hospital tomorrow."

"If you're busy…"

He shrugged. "I was going to pay bills and watch a game. Nothing urgent."

"Okay. Thanks."

Chapter Twenty-One

The truck lurched forward, then hopped like a bunny before the engine died with a sputter. Matilda shoved her foot down on the brake.

"More acceleration, lift the clutch slowly." Ryan's voice was soft, gentle. He hadn't lost his temper with her once even though she'd stalled the truck about a hundred times so far.

They'd only made it halfway around the lake, and yet it'd taken them forty-five minutes. "I'm sorry I'm so slow."

"Fine by me. It's not an easy road to navigate with all the hills and turns. Plus, you can't drive real fast on here, which makes it more likely you'll stall. You're getting the hang of it though."

She hadn't expected him to be so encouraging, it made her feel a little less stressed about the whole situation. Perhaps she'd taken on more than she should. She might not be in the country long, why bother learning to drive Rita's truck? But with Rita out of action it would probably help for her to be mobile—she could do the grocery shopping and run errands for her. That's if Rita needed it. She still wasn't sure what it would look like when Rita came home.

The drive around the lake was picturesque. A lot of the houses were small and old with rundown boat sheds and weathered docks. But some were, like Ryan's house, new or renovated, big and imposing. The lakeside community was a mixture of folks from all different backgrounds.

"What made you choose to live here?" Matilda pushed the gear stick back into first and started the engine.

"I used to come here to visit my grandpa as a kid. He's passed on now, and my parents sold his property. But I decided that when I could afford it, I'd buy somewhere nearby. I used to love our outings on the pontoon boat or fishing off the dock. Some of my favourite childhood memories."

"I like that," she replied. "It's a little bit like our place in Kingscliff. My parents built it when I was young, and they lived there the rest of their lives. It's special to all of us because of that. I love it there, it feels like home. I can really relax when I'm home."

"I'm impressed you travelled to the other side of the world by yourself on a hunch. Rita told me you're looking for family."

"Yeah, I'm not sure if it's impressive or if it's silly. But either way, here I am. And I'm having a blast. I had no idea how it would go, but I've already made some great friendships."

They made their way slowly back to the lake house as it grew dark outside. The truck lurched to a stop, and then rolled forwards.

Ryan put his hand over hers on the gear stick. "Put it in first before you switch it off."

Electricity jolted up her arm at his touch. She shifted the gear, then added the handbrake, her face warm. He released her hand, and she pulled it away.

"Do you still want to visit Rita tomorrow?" she asked.

He nodded. "I'll be at work until about four. I can drive you after that."

"Sounds good. In the meantime, I'll keep practicing around the lake myself."

He climbed out of the truck. "Work that clutch."

As he walked away, she sat silently in the cab, her heart pumping hard. What had just happened?

Chapter Twenty-Two

At four p.m. the next day, Matilda patiently waited inside the lake house for Ryan to get home from work. She'd spent the morning driving the truck around the quiet lake road. Her driving skills had improved substantially, and she'd only stalled the vehicle once this time.

A few minutes later he pulled into the driveway. She hurried out to climb into his truck. He wore jeans and a buttoned brown jacket. His hair was mussed from where he'd likely worn some kind of hat, but it was nowhere to be seen now.

"Hi," she said.

He backed out of the drive. "Sorry I'm a little late."

"No worries. How was work?"

"Fine. How about you? Did you drive some more?"

She nodded. "I think I'm getting better at it."

After he pulled onto the highway, he spoke again. "I was thinking about what you said yesterday. About your visa."

"Uh huh?" She couldn't imagine why he would be thinking about her at all, let alone her immigration status.

"What if we were married?"

She almost fell out of her seat. "What?"

His brow furrowed. He glanced at her. "We could pretend, you know? You could get a green card."

She stared at him with wide eyes. "Do you even understand what you're saying? That's not something you should be flippant about."

He shrugged. "It's no big deal. Nothing has to change. We pretend we're married. You get a visa."

"But we would have to actually *be* married. We can't simply pretend, the IRS would know if we're legally married or not."

"Yeah, I get it. We have to do the paperwork, but it wouldn't be real."

"I think they investigate that."

"Really?" He arched an eyebrow.

"Yeah, really."

"Well, I guess we could pretend we were together. That way, they wouldn't be able to find anything against us."

"That sounds like a lot of work."

"Can you get a visa any other way?"

She'd looked into it all afternoon. There were no visas that she qualified for. "No, I can't."

"Well then," he said as though the matter was settled.

"Why would you want to do that for me?"

"It might get my parents off my back about dating. They're always on me about finding someone. Apparently, I'm ancient and they'll never get grandchildren. Plus, I've got this high school reunion coming up. It was supposed to be fifteen years but we postponed it to this year. I don't want to go by myself. I like the idea of taking a wife."

"You want me to go to your high school reunion as your wife?" She couldn't believe what she was hearing. She thought he despised her. Or at the very least had complete disdain for her.

"I don't want to face all those questions. What happened to your wife? Why are you single? What's wrong with you?" He ran fingers through his hair, making it look spiky. His jaw clenched.

"You were married?"

"You're full of questions tonight, aren't you?" He glanced at her with irritation on his face.

"I'm sorry. You just suggested something absolutely crazy. I'm trying to catch up."

"It'd solve both our problems, right? You'd get your visa. I'd dodge all the hard questions. It's a win-win."

"It's a bit extreme."

"If you don't want to do it, just say so."

"It's not that..."

"So, you're in?"

She laughed. "I guess so." This was crazy. They were both out of their minds. She barely knew him. But it was just a document. It wasn't like they were actually going to be a married couple. And they could get an annulment if it didn't work out. "Let's get married."

* * *

When they arrived at the hospital, Rita had her bag packed up and was about to call an Uber to get home. She was delighted to see them.

"You two are angels," she said with hands raised high. "I can't believe you're here."

"I wanted to surprise you," Matilda said. "What's going on? Are you going home already?"

"I've already done the paperwork. Unfortunately, Julie had to get back to school last night, so she couldn't drive me home today. And I didn't think to ask you since you can't drive."

Matilda offered her an arm to lean on while Ryan carried her bag. "Ryan's been teaching me. I hope that's okay. I used your truck."

"Oh, wonderful. That's so kind of you, Ryan. You're always thinking of others, you can't help yourself."

Matilda was surprised to hear Rita's assessment of her neighbour. She was beginning to realise she'd had a wrong first impression of the man.

By the time they got home, Matilda was starving. She hadn't eaten dinner and lunch had been a long time ago. She and Ryan helped Rita inside with her things. Then she walked him back out to his fence line. She stood, hands on hips, watching him walk through the gate that joined the two properties together.

"Thanks for tonight. And for the driving lesson yesterday."

"No problem."

"Are you serious about the marriage thing?"

He turned to look at her. "I am if you are."

"It might help. I'm going to the social security office next week to see if I can get a card. If I can do that, I'll be able to work."

"We should go to the registry office before that and get hitched." He grinned. "My parents are going to freak."

"My sister will kill me. I'm not going to tell her. There's really no reason."

"What will Rita think?"

"I don't know. She'll probably say we've lost our minds."

He offered her a weak smile. "She'd be right about that."

They both laughed awkwardly.

"Okay, well, good night then. I guess I'll see you soon."

"Oh, by the way, the reunion is on Friday night."

"Next week is going to be busy then. Wedding, social security card, new job, and a high school reunion."

He shut the gate. "Sleep well."

As she walked back into the house, she couldn't stop thinking about what he'd said. They'd be married by this time next week. She couldn't wrap her mind around it. It didn't make sense—she wasn't the type to do anything impulsive. And yet lately, that's all she'd done. Or maybe she was impulsive, but she'd never really allowed herself to be free to act on those impulses because that wasn't what her family did. They were all cautious, careful, made studied and informed decisions.

"Don't rush into anything," her father used to always say. "Take your time, think it through."

Good advice in general. But it'd held her back from doing so many things she'd wanted to do. And now that restraint was gone, was she going overboard? She stepped inside, leaned against the wall, and squeezed her eyes shut to remember his face. It was still there, in her mind's eye, as clear as though he was standing in front of her. That would fade, she knew. Her mother's face was a vague memory now, but Dad was still large as life. In her imagination, she fell into his arms and he raised them around her to pull her into a bear hug. It was her safe place, and she immediately felt tears spring to her eyes.

"I miss you, Dad. I need you to help me with these decisions. I want to stay and get to know my family better, find the truth about my roots. But to do that, I'm going to have to marry a man I don't know. Is that ridiculous? Should I just give up and go home?"

She knew the answer immediately. She wasn't ready to turn back yet. This journey wasn't over. She trudged to the kitchen to look for something to eat, resolute in her decision.

Chapter Twenty-Three

Their wedding was short and simple. They told Rita their plans, and she came as their witness. She told them she thought they were doing it all wrong, but she didn't intend to stand in their way since they were grown adults. They signed the paperwork down at the county probate court. There was no waiting period, so they both thought they might as well get married today as any other day.

He wore a pair of jeans and the ever-present, brown-buttoned jacket. He took off his hat for the ceremony, and his light brown curls remained hat shaped. She wore a long white skirt and a white sweater with red deer printed on the front of it. It was the only white outfit she'd bought. So, it would have to do.

He held her hand as they walked into the office and kept hold of it throughout the ceremony. When it came time for the rings, he surprised her by presenting two plain gold bands. Hers was a little big on her finger, but it felt good.

As she vowed to spend her life with this man she'd only recently met, to love and honour, cherish and keep him for all her days, Matilda experienced a twinge of shame that she didn't mean the words. But if it meant she could stay with Rita and get to know her family better, discover her roots, she was willing to cross her fingers and say the words. At least for now. It wouldn't last—she knew that. But she still couldn't believe he was willing to go through with it. All he asked in return was that she pretended to be his wife to his family and at the reunion. And since she *was* his wife, at least officially, she figured it wouldn't take too much pretending on her part.

She twisted the ring round and round her finger as they left the courthouse. She'd have to get it resized.

She never imagined this is how her wedding would go. She'd dreamed of this moment since she was twenty-three, imagining how Cam would pop the question, what she'd wear, what he'd say in his speech at the reception. But two years later, they were broken up and now she'd gone and married a stranger at a courthouse on the other side of the world.

None of it seemed real.

After their wedding, he drove her to a tiny rural social security office about an hour away in Monroe. She took the marriage certificate and her passport and went in alone. There was no one else there other than the man sitting behind the counter. There was a glass partition between them, so she leaned forward to speak to him.

"Um ... hi, I need to get a social security number."

"You got your paperwork?" he asked as he chewed on a toothpick.

She nodded, pushed the papers and her passport beneath the divider where there was a smooth metal slot.

He took the paperwork and looked it over. "Says here you're on a tourist visa."

Her stomach clenched. "That's right, but I got married to an American today. And I'll be applying for a green card. The problem is, I really need to get a job and have an income, and I don't know how long the green card will take to process. It might be up to a year." That's what she'd read online. The thought of waiting that long made her anxious. She couldn't last a year living on her savings.

The man frowned at her paperwork, looked over her marriage certificate, then offered her a warm smile. "Well, I guess we'd better get you a social security number then, sweetheart."

She walked out of the office with the new paper card in her hand and held it up for Ryan to see as she approached the truck.

He slapped his thigh and laughed when she climbed into the truck. "I can't believe you did it. I thought this place would be your best bet, since I doubt they've ever met an Aussie in their lives. And that accent of yours most likely did the trick."

"The man working behind the counter was so kind. He hardly asked me any questions and handed over the card just like that." She snapped her fingers.

"Ah, what a beautiful and secure system we have," he said as he started the engine.

Matilda chatted his ear off as they drove home. He interjected occasionally, but she couldn't seem to stop herself from talking—she felt so comfortable with him. He was a good listener. And she'd clearly misjudged him from their first interactions. He wasn't a big talker, but he was kind, patient and easy to talk to. And she found herself telling him all about her breakup with Cam, the DNA test, the discoveries she'd made, and her hopes and plans for the future.

By the time they'd made it home, she wished they had a little longer to drive so she could ask him more questions about his own life. He didn't offer much in the way of information, and he seemed like such a mystery to her. She still knew very little about him.

"I'll pick you up at six for the reunion," he said as they both climbed out of the truck.

"What should I wear?"

"I don't know ... I'm wearing jeans."

"Jeans?"

"The theme is *County Fair*. So I guess you should dress like you're going to the fair." He leaned against the truck's side, crossed his legs.

"Sounds fun."

He arched an eyebrow. "We'll see."

"Bye, husband."

"Huh? Oh yeah ... right. Glad I could get you that social security number. Don't break the law now, okay?"

"Devo, I was going to rob a bank. Now I'll have to come up with some other way to fund my lifestyle. Don't worry, I'll be a goodie-two shoes."

"A goodie what now?"

She laughed. "Never mind ... no bank robbery, I promise. I won't bolt or flip, I'm fair dinkum." She offered him a mock salute.

"Y'all crack yourselves up with that kind of talk, no doubt." He crossed his arms over his thick chest, his brow furrowed in confusion.

"We do like to have a giggle."

"I genuinely have no idea what you're talking about, but you're cute, I'll give you that."

She grunted. "Well, *tah* for that. The feeling is entirely mutual. See ya."

* * *

At five after six, there was a knock at the door. Matilda took one last glance in the mirror. She'd put her hair in a high pony-tail and styled her makeup to be fun and colourful. She wore a blue puffer jacket with a blue sweater beneath it, and a pair of jeans and white joggers. The blue of the sweater brought out her eyes, and she'd highlighted the combination with blue eyeliner. She quickly sprayed herself with perfume, then grabbed her purse and headed for the door.

The hat hair was gone. Ryan had showered and combed his hair so that it had the perfectly mussed look and was still a little damp. He smelled delicious, and she had to press a smile to her face and hold her breath so that she didn't sink into his arms right there on the stoop.

"Ready to go?" he asked.

She nodded. If she said a word right now she'd give herself away.

He walked to the truck and opened the door for her, then held her hand to help her step up into the passenger seat. Her heart hammered against her ribcage. She wanted to swoon. But swooning right now would give the wrong impression. He was her fake husband, not her real husband. She had to keep the facts in mind. It would be pointless to develop real feelings in a pretend relationship. He was doing her a favour and helping himself at the same time. Besides, she barely knew him. Better to keep things professional.

"Thank you," she murmured.

He shut the door and went around to the other side. They listened to the radio on the way to the reunion. She was surprisingly quiet. His gallantry and aftershave had made her weak at the knees and she didn't trust herself to speak.

"Not much to say tonight, huh?" he asked with a glance in her direction.

"Not really." She couldn't say what she was thinking. It was completely inappropriate. Instead, she looked out the window and tried to count the trees whizzing by. Anything to distract herself from the intoxicating scent and the freshly laundered and very masculine man seated next to her. She turned up the radio and hummed quietly to the music.

They arrived at Newton High School and pulled into the parking lot. She hadn't realised they'd be celebrating at the high school. But that made sense and was kind of exciting for her, given she'd only ever seen American high schools in the movies. As she fixed her lipstick in the mirror, she was surprised by Ryan at the door, opening it for her and holding out a hand to help her step down. She'd never been treated this way by a man before and wasn't sure how to respond.

Then he held up his arm and she slid her hand through the crook. He looked down at her with a grunt. "We're married, you know. Gotta at least give it a bit of realism."

"Right, I almost forgot. Should we set any rules before we go in?"

His eyes narrowed. "Rules?"

"Yeah, like no kissing on the lips, no handsy touching, that kind of thing."

"Oh, right. Gotcha."

"Anything to add?"

"Not really. I'm fine with you getting handsy. If that's your thing." His eyes sparkled with mischief.

She shook her head. "Uh, thanks, but I think I'll be able to restrain myself." Not exactly the truth, given how she'd felt on the ride over, but she wasn't about to give him the satisfaction of knowing how much he'd unsettled her.

They had to give their names at a desk draped in a red tablecloth. A quick look into the gym behind the woman handing them name badges revealed it to be just like the movies. Matilda couldn't wipe the grin from her face.

"What are you so happy about?" Ryan asked as he pinned on his name badge.

"I feel like I've stepped onto a movie set."

He frowned. "It's a high school gym."

"I know, isn't it great?"

"You don't have this in Australia?"

"Not really. We have grass. Fields. Open air schools. No hallways or cafeterias. Sometimes there's a basketball court."

"You just walk around outside?"

"That's right. Kids wander around the school grounds, out in the open. No gates, no metal detectors, no locks."

"Sounds ... nice."

"It is. But this is fun. I'm geeking out just a little bit."

"Well, geek out over by the drinks table because I need a drink." He reached for her hand.

"Good idea." She followed his lead.

They bought two plastic cups filled with some kind of spiked punch, then headed over to where the round tables were set up to mingle. Matilda and Ryan put their jackets on the backs of two chairs. Matilda was trying to decide whether to sit first or check out the food tables. The gym was decorated with bales of hay, brightly festooned with ribbons and hanging signs announcing things like *Win a prize for the best shot, Piglet race,* and *Calf wrestling - best of three!*

The first person to approach them was a woman with red hair. Her brilliantly white teeth accentuated by a black light in the corner were the first thing Matilda noticed. She hurried towards them with a wide smile, her purple dress swishing around her thin frame.

"Well, hello there, Ryan Merritt! It's been so long. How're y'all doing?"

Ryan seemed surprised by her embrace and took a step backwards to steady himself. He cleared his throat. "Uh, Meghan, it's nice to see you. I guess it's been at least five years or so."

Meghan squeezed Ryan's bicep, her smile never fading. "You're just getting better and better with age. You big ole hunk, you!"

155

Her gaze turned to focus on Matilda. "And who is this?"

"This is my wife, Matilda."

Her smile faded. "Wife? I didn't hear you got married."

"It's new," Matilda said with a shy smile. She stepped closer to Ryan and threaded her hand through his arm. He patted her hand.

"Yep, she's the missus. The old ball and chain. I'm done for."

Matilda glared at him.

He coughed. "I mean, she's the one I've been searching for my whole life. She makes me so happy."

Meghan's eyes narrowed as she studied Matilda. "Well, how about that?" She shouted to a group of women huddled around the fried pickle stand. "Y'all come over here!"

The women scurried over and hummed around Ryan like a hive of bees.

"Ryan, you look so handsome."

"I can't believe you're not taller than you were in high school. You seem taller."

"How's your momma, Ryan? My mom said to tell her hi."

Matilda took a few steps back to get out of their way as they crowded around him. She set her hands on her hips and watched.

Ryan raised his hands in surrender. "Whoa! One at a time. Hi, y'all. It's good to see you. I want you to meet my wife. This is Matilda."

The group spun, as one, to survey her, taking her in from head to toe with a single glance.

"That's right, he's married," Meghan added, in a sickly-sweet tone. "He's finally off the market."

As Ryan answered the barrage of questions aimed his way, Meghan turned her attention to Matilda.

"My parents stay in touch with Ryan's. And according to them, only last month, he was as single as a Pringle."

Matilda shrugged. "Maybe they were mistaken."

"I don't think so. You say y'all are married?"

"That's right." She held up her left hand to show Meghan the ring.

"Where's the diamond?"

"We prefer simple," Matilda replied.

"Huh."

"Were you and Ryan friends in high school?"

Meghan crossed her arms and spun to look at Ryan while she spoke. "You could say that, I suppose. We spent time together."

"Did you date?"

"All through senior year."

"Oh really? He never mentioned you."

Meghan's keen eyes were fixed once again on Matilda's face. Green and catlike, they didn't miss a thing. "Never? I wonder why."

"I don't know. Perhaps he didn't think to say anything."

"Well, you certainly hit the jackpot."

Matilda frowned. "What do you mean?"

"He's tall, handsome, wealthy, and kind. What more could a girl want? I hope you deserve him."

"Wealthy? I'm not sure I'd call him wealthy." He was a handyman who lived on Jackson Lake. His house was admittedly quite nice but certainly not a mansion. And he was doing it up himself. Would a wealthy man do that?

"He owns the biggest construction company in several counties. I'd consider that wealthy."

"He owns.... Of course. You're right. He's clearly wealthy." Matilda stumbled over the words. She'd give them away if she wasn't careful. They had to believe she and Ryan were married, or she'd have failed to uphold her end of the deal. He'd done so much for her, helping her. The least she could do is not put her foot in it.

Meghan eyed her suspiciously. "You sound like you have no idea what he does for a living."

Matilda laughed nervously. "Do I? How funny. I can be such a ditz."

She grabbed Ryan by the arm and pulled him away from the crowd of women. "Come on, honey, let's get some fried things. The Oreos, cheese sticks, and Snickers bars look interesting. I'm dying to try them. And what on earth is funnel cake?"

He stumbled after her, then pulled her close so that she was pressed up against his chest. He looked deep into her eyes then leaned down to kiss her on the tip of her nose, ever so gently. It sent a tremor through her.

"Thank you for rescuing me," he whispered.

"You're welcome," she replied.

They marched off together, hand in hand, towards the foot stalls.

Chapter Twenty-Four

TWENTY-FIVE YEARS AGO

Helen sat in the rocking chair by the nursery window. She stared through the panes at the American flag waving in the wind. The clink of the metal hook holding the bottom of the flag against the flagpole was a rhythmic irritation that made her skin crawl.

He was gone.

Paul had been killed in a bombing raid on his base. It'd happened eight months earlier. And yet she still couldn't quite believe it. She rested her arms across her swollen belly. Wriggled her fat toes. She was retaining water. Lots of it. It seemed to her as though she'd gained about fifty pounds. But she was certain a good bit of it was oedema since when she crossed her legs for longer than thirty seconds, she left a massive dent in the bottom leg where the top one had rested.

But she couldn't bring herself to care. All she'd wanted for the past months was to have a hole open up in the ground and swallow her. She didn't want to go on. Didn't want to face life on her own with a child. But she had no choice. Her body continued doing what it was designed to do. The pregnancy had gone well for the most part. She'd been pretty sick for about six months but lately had begun to feel better. And now with the swelling, she was ready for it to be over.

"Just come out already," she whispered to her stomach. "It's about time, and I don't mind if you're a little early. A few days won't matter."

She stroked a circle on her stomach and felt the baby kick. It wasn't really a kick, the baby rolled over and she watched as her stomach distended into the shape of an elbow that moved around beneath her dress. She would never get used to that. It was so special and yet strange at the same time. She picked up her journal and read the last line she'd written.

I'm waiting for you to join me, little one. But I don't have much of a heart left to give you. I hope you'll understand.

How could she be a good mother when she'd been shattered into pieces? The one thing she'd been so afraid of had finally happened. Paul was gone. She'd never see him again. Never be held in his arms. Never hear his voice or laugh with him. The house would be empty, her bed cold. She would never forgive the world for taking him from her.

It made no sense that she could keep on living, but she didn't have a choice. No one knew how she felt. She'd faced the funeral, the conversations, the condolences, and her work since his death with a stoic smile on her face. But it wasn't real. It was a mask she wore so that she didn't have to put up with people's pity, so that she wouldn't have to face their questions, their concerns, and their well-meaning interruptions in her empty, fruitless life.

The phone rang. She picked it up and forced herself to sound cheery. "Hello?"

"Hey, honey, it's Rita. How are you feeling?"

"I'm fine, Rita. Fine."

Her voice sounded empty, cold, to her ears. But maybe Rita wouldn't notice. Helen had gotten good at hiding.

Rita hesitated. "Okay, that's great. The countdown is on, huh? You ready?"

"Ready as I'll ever be." She'd taken to speaking in cliches and sayings, people seemed to like it, and it meant she didn't have to really think about anything deep. Was she ready? She couldn't probe that particular wellspring of emotion right now, so a cliche was all she had to give.

Just then, a pain pressed down on her abdomen like a strong muscle cramp. She gasped, eyes widening. What was that?

"Are you okay?"

"I don't know." She stood up and fluid gushed between her legs, wetting her skin, dress, and the carpet at her feet. "Oh no!"

"What is it? Helen?"

"I think my water just broke. It's so gross. The carpet is all wet and I had this room perfectly clean and ready for the baby!" Her voice broke into a wail as she pressed her feet up and down on the increasingly sodden carpet.

"That doesn't matter. I'll clean it up for you, honey. Don't you worry about it. Now, why don't you head to your bathroom and get in the tub. You've already planned to labor there, right? I'll be there in fifteen minutes, and I'll help you."

Helen hung up the phone and waddled to the bathroom off her master bedroom. She couldn't walk properly anymore since her hips had shifted. For the past week, it'd felt as though her uterus was going to fall out, which put pressure on her hips and made her walk like a duck.

She stared at the tub, all ready to go with candles around the outside, books stacked at one end, a box of chocolates, and a speaker for music. There was no way she was getting in that tub—she might not be able to get out again. Already her legs were cramping so badly, she could barely stand. What had she been thinking?

Instead, she grabbed a few towels from the bathroom rack and carried them to her bed, laid them out and then climbed onto them. She lay on her back, legs bent up and stared at the ceiling. That was better. The cramping stopped.

Fifteen minutes later, she heard Rita opening the back door with her spare key.

"Hello? Helen! I'm here!" Her sister bounded up the stairs.

She found Helen on the bed.

"Are you okay, honey? You're not in the tub?"

Another contraction wracked her body, making her grimace with pain. "No, not getting in the tub. Might not be able to climb out again, and what if I fall?"

"Good point," Rita replied. "I'll get you a chair if you like. Or are you fine on the bed?"

"A chair would be good. There's a nerve pinching in my lower back, and I'm losing feeling in one leg."

"That's not okay. Here you go." Rita helped her into a chair and for the next five hours, the two of them alternated between her sitting on the chair with Rita massaging various parts of her body—feet, shoulders, arms, legs. And then she'd take a turn pacing or rocking on hands and knees until the cramping in her legs forced her back onto the bed.

She couldn't eat a single chocolate. But she did sip some ice water.

Finally, it was time to go to the hospital, the contractions were close together and she was experiencing a lot more pain.

Rita drove her there and then stayed with her while she was examined and went through the final stages of labour.

Helen felt herself disappear into a deep place within herself. She focused so hard that she only opened her eyes to push when the doctor told her to. The rest of the time she was looking inward, not thinking about anything but simply existing in that place.

When things started to go wrong, she knew it right away. She felt it happen. There was something wrong. Panic overtook her, and her breathing accelerated. The monitors she and the baby were attached to began beeping. Helen's eyes flew open, and she looked at the doctor.

"We're going to have to deliver this baby now," the doctor said calmly.

And that was the last thing Helen remembered.

* * *

When she woke, she was in a darkened room alone. A monitor beeped rhythmically beside her. She glanced at it. It was her heart rate, but the baby monitor wasn't there any longer. Her mouth was dry. She tried to sit up, but her whole body hurt and her head felt light. She tried to speak, but her voice wouldn't work.

There was a glass of water with a straw on the table beside her bed. She reached for it and took a sip, then cleared her throat and tried again.

"Hello? Anyone?"

A nurse hurried into the room, her white shoes making barely a sound on the tiled floor.

"There you are. How are you feeling?" The nurse walked over to the side of her bed and began to take her pulse. She smiled warmly at Helen.

"I'm okay," Helen croaked. "What happened? Where's the baby?"

"You experienced pre-eclampsia. Your organs were shutting down, so we had to do an emergency cesarean. Your baby is in the special care nursery for now, but she will be glad to see you."

"She? I had a girl?"

"You had a girl." The nurse beamed. "I'll get you something to eat and then I'll take you to see her if you like."

"Thank you," Helen said. "My sister?"

"She's just gone home for a shower, I think. She's been here for days."

"Days? I was out for days?"

The nurse's smile faded. "You almost didn't make it. We've had you sedated. But you're doing better today."

"How has the baby managed for that long without me?"

"We've been bottle feeding her formula. Your sister's been a big help. She hasn't wanted to leave the baby's side. Or yours, for that matter. Your parents were here too. I'm sure they'll be back shortly."

Helen ate some jello and custard. Her stomach felt fine, but the nurse said she should take it slow. So she drank some hot tea, and then the nurse pushed her wheelchair down the hallway to the nursery.

She felt better after eating and drinking something, but her whole body was weak and hurt. They reached the special care nursery, and her heart rate accelerated. Where was her baby? The nursery was quiet and in semi-darkness. There were small cribs dotted about the space, some with machinery and monitors attached. The nurse led her to a small crib with a tiny baby laying on her back, swaddled in a white cloth with pink stripes.

"Is this her?"

The nurse gave a nod. She picked the baby up and lay her gently in Helen's arms.

She'd almost dreaded this moment. How would she feel? Would she love this child who'd been left behind by her father? Or would she resent her? Would she ever be able to bond? Or be happy again?

But the moment she laid eyes on her child, her heart leapt inside of her. Love for this helpless little creature swamped her until her eyes brimmed with tears.

"She's beautiful," she whispered, as she reached a finger towards the baby's tiny, clenched fist. The fist unclenched and closed around her finger.

Her little face was perfect, with long, dark eyelashes, a wisp of dark hair, and rosebud lips.

"She's very healthy and doesn't need to stay here in the nursery if you're ready to take her back to your room and breastfeed. I can help you with that."

Helen gave a nod. The nurse pushed them back to the room.

When they arrived, Rita was there looking anxious. She gave a shout of relief at the sight of them and hurried to squat beside Helen, her eyes glistening. "You're okay. You gave me such a fright."

"I'm sorry," Helen said, her voice breaking. "Isn't she amazing?"

"She's perfect. But I thought I was going to lose you." Tears streaked down Rita's cheeks as she gazed into Helen's eyes.

Helen reached for her hand and squeezed it. "I'm here, and I'm fine."

"Are you really?"

"Yes, I am. And I'm deliriously happy for the first time in a very long time."

Rita wiped her tears away with a laugh. "Well, that's music to my ears."

"She looks nothing like you. She must take after Paul. What will you call her?"

"Her name is Julie. Because she's so perfect and innocent. The world will never be able to hurt her, I won't let it." Helen gazed at her baby's face.

"What a lovely name." Rita stood up and sighed. "It's time for a new beginning. For all of us."

"Yes, it's time." Helen agreed. And she meant it.

Chapter Twenty-Five

The cafe was relatively quiet, which gave Rita a chance to relax. She sat in her tiny office in front of the computer, a cup of coffee in hand, peering out the back window at the small courtyard. Winter was over, and spring had begun with a few tiny green shoots on the honeysuckle vine that covered the trellis over the courtyard. It was a month since Matilda had married Ryan. And even though she'd been against it, she had to admit it hadn't changed anything about their lives. The two of them still lived separately, although they were spending more and more time together. He'd taught Matilda to drive, so now she was able to transport herself around the county. And he'd taken her to meet his family.

Rita had wondered how that would go, but it seems Matilda hit it off with his mother and they'd become fast friends. She didn't want to remind Matilda that the relationship wasn't real and she had every chance of breaking his poor mother's heart when it ended. No one wanted to hear her point of view on the subject. They were young and impetuous

167

and they'd do whatever they wanted to do. She still thought it was naive and careless, and bound to end in tears.

But instead of ruminating on that particular subject while she stared into the back garden, she was thinking about Julie's birth, all those years ago. And how scared she'd been at the prospect of losing Helen. She'd thought several times that she would have to raise Julie for her sister. But in the end, Helen had pulled through and hadn't died until Julie was an adult. So, although Rita had done her best since to be there for her niece, she didn't need her as much as she might've if the labor and delivery had gone differently. And for that she was grateful, on Julie's behalf as well as her own. Every moment they got to share of this life had been a blessing.

There was a knock at her office door, and Rita spun on her office chair to see cousin Cathy Lambert standing there in a bright turquoise leisure suit with a matching headband. Her blue eyeshadow offset her eyes, which were narrowed to go along with her scowl.

"There you are, Rita. Daydreaming again, I see."

"How nice of you to drop by, Cathy. Can I help you with something?"

Cathy took a seat without being asked. She sat with a ramrod straight back and picked at her long, painted fingernails. "I need to talk to you about the cafe."

"Oh?"

"You know Uncle Ray and Daddy built this place together?"

"Of course, I know the story well."

"And when Daddy left, he and Uncle Ray had an agreement."

"What kind of agreement?" Rita asked as she leaned forward to better focus on her cousin's words.

Cathy cleared her throat. "They agreed that when they

passed, the cafe would go to their first borns. Both first borns. To be shared."

"Hmmm…"

"That's you and me, Rita. And both Uncle Ray and Daddy have passed. Which means, this cafe is just as much mine as it is yours."

* * *

Rita crossed her arms and glared at her cousin. "Cathy, what on earth are you talking about?"

"You know it's true," Cathy continued. "We're supposed to be running this place together. But you never let me get a leg in."

"It's my cafe," Rita replied, indignantly. How dare Cathy waltz in here after all these years of Rita slaving away to keep the doors of the Honeysuckle Cafe open and claim a share of ownership. It was just like her.

"It belongs to both of us."

"Do you have any documentation that proves it?" Rita asked.

Cathy's eyes narrowed. "Do you have any to prove your ownership?"

Rita blanched at that. It was well known her father hadn't left a will. Much to the dismay of the entire family. But so far, no one had questioned his estate. When Helen was alive, she hadn't wanted the cafe or the house. But she had inherited their savings as her portion. Which had now gone to Julie to pay her way through college and help put a downpayment on an apartment when the time came.

Cathy looked smug. "You have no proof of inheritance. And I've spoken to my lawyer. She thinks I have a chance to win back my share."

"Uncle Bill walked away from the cafe. He gave up any rights to the business when he did that."

"You know why he walked away," Cathy spat, as she stood to her feet. "You've got no right to throw that back in my face when you're to blame for it all, anyway."

"I'm to blame? That's rich." Rita stood to her feet, her heart thundering in anger as adrenaline surged through her veins. "You know what I've been through. And for you to come in here and try to make my life even more difficult than it's already been is just ... well, it's typical of you. You don't care about anyone but yourself."

She'd lost a husband, a sister and both parents in a short space of time. The whole family knew what she'd endured and how much grief she'd experienced in her life. Most of them had compassion on her, but not Cathy.

"We've all been through things, Rita. But that doesn't change the facts. And the fact is, this place is as much mine as it is yours. And it's time I claimed my ownership stake in the business. You'll be hearing from my lawyer."

She stomped out of the office, slamming the door shut behind her. The sound reverberated through the cafe. The cafe manager, Amanda, popped the door open a few moments later looking worried.

"Are you okay, Rita? What was all that about?"

Rita sank into her chair with a sigh. "Just my greedy, selfish cousin doing what she can to bring on a heart attack. Nothing for you to worry about." She chuckled. "Life never stops handing out lemons, does it?"

Amanda shook her head with a frown. "Doesn't seem like it. Do you want me to chase her down and kick her butt for you?"

Rita laughed. "Not this time. Maybe next time though, so rain check?"

Amanda grinned. "You got it."

Chapter Twenty-Six

Rita sat on the examination table in a gown that was open in the back. Her feet didn't touch the ground and swung back and forth in place. The door opened and the doctor entered. She'd been Rita's doctor for fifteen years and they knew each other well. They attended pilates together. At least they had a decade earlier. Rita didn't make it to pilates classes very often these days.

"So?" Rita asked.

Dr Gilmore had already run every test known to mankind. Surely they'd found what was going on.

With a sigh, the doctor sat in her chair. She swivelled to face Rita who was suddenly very aware of the fact that she was almost naked and seated like a small child with her feet swinging. She pressed both hands to the table, ready to climb down, then the doctor spoke.

"You know how you told me you've been having some difficulty swallowing?"

"Right, but it's not that big a deal. I'm sure I'm just imagining things. It doesn't happen all the time."

Dr Gilmore nodded. "I'm afraid there's a little more to it than that."

"What is it?" Rita's heart dropped.

"It seems you've got an oesophageal growth."

"A what now?"

"In your oesophagus. There's a growth."

"You think it's cancer?"

The doctor leaned forward slightly. "Our tests show it is cancerous."

Rita gasped, held her breath. Cancer? She was too young for this. Only fifty-eight years of age. That was nothing. She had decades left. Surely. This couldn't be happening.

"We'll treat it, and we'll deal with it. Okay?" Dr Gilmore's eyes were steel. Her voice was soft.

"I thought I only had to worry about my heart. I'm taking the medication, I'm walking more often. I was doing everything right." Rita stared at the floor. "How could this happen?"

"You didn't cause this, Rita," Dr Gilmore replied. "You're not a smoker. Or a big drinker."

"I hardly ever have a drink," Rita agreed.

"It's not something you did. These things happen. But we've gotten pretty good at treating cancer these days. There are plenty of treatment options available, and I'm going to refer you to an incredible oncologist."

"You won't treat me?" Rita looked up, tears filling her eyes.

"No, I'll still be here, and you can consult with me anytime you like. But you need a specialist for this, Rita. That's not me."

"Okay."

"And what I'd like you to do right now is go directly to the hospital and check in. I'll let them know you're coming, and I'll ask the oncologist to meet you there. I want her to go through all your test results and do whatever else she needs to do to put a plan together for your treatment. Okay?"

"What's the rush?" Rita was puzzled. This wasn't how doctors normally handled these things. There were waiting lists and appointments.

"I'm concerned about the chest pain you reported. I need to ensure that we're taking good care of your heart through all of this. It might be fine. It could be a symptom of the growth. Or it might mean there's something wrong with your heart. But we won't know without further testing. I'll also get your cardiologist involved. But it will mean a night in the hospital."

"Wow." Rita didn't know what to say. She was supposed to be hosting a party at the cafe that evening.

"Whatever you're thinking about, it can wait," Dr Gilmore stated. "This is your focus now. You need all your energy to get well."

"You're right," Rita replied. "Okay, I'll drive to the hospital. It'll be fine. It's all going to be fine." She said the words like a mantra, willing them to be true.

Chapter Twenty-Seven

It was her first *Spring Fling* at the Honeysuckle Cafe, and Matilda was excited to participate. She'd worked at the cafe for almost a month, and she felt like she had a good handle on how things operated. It'd been years since she'd waited tables. A job at a local Thai restaurant had helped pay her way through university. But the muscle memory remained even after all these years, she found herself quickly slipping back into the role.

She tied a bright blue apron around her waist and checked her lipstick in the hallway mirror that hung between the dining room and the outside courtyard. They'd had the courtyard closed for winter, but now that it was officially spring, it was open, and a cool breeze floated in every time someone pushed through the swinging doors.

Outside, birds sang. There was greenery working its way out of the earth and the sky overhead was a deep blue with only a few white fluffy clouds scooting by.

Matilda felt happy.

She put vases on the tables and then filled each one with a single cut white flower. Then, she set out silverware and napkins. Refilled the ketchup and mustard bottles. And made certain the salt and pepper shakers were ready to go.

Before long it was time to open the cafe. But there was no sign of Rita. Matilda frowned, her hands on hips, and looked from the front door to the office. She marched to the office, but Rita wasn't there. Then, she pulled out her phone and called Rita. But there was no answer. She left a voicemail, then with a sigh, hurried to open the front door herself. There'd be customers lined up outside soon, so she'd better let them in. Rita would understand. Although it wasn't like her to be late. Where could she be?

Amanda poked her head out of the kitchen. "Everything good to go?"

"I can't find Rita," Matilda replied.

"Never mind. I'm sure she's on her way. She called me earlier but I missed it and she left me a message but I can't figure out what she was saying. It's all garbled, keeps cutting out."

"Maybe she was calling to tell us she'll be late. Well, we're ready to go anyway. The food smells delicious."

"I'm pretty proud of the BBQ pulled pork and slow cooked beef brisket," Amanda replied. "I think people will be happy. Have you tried the Brunswick stew yet?"

Matilda shook her head.

"Well, come a get a bite before things get going. You don't want to be starving all evening long."

Matilda joined Amanda and the kitchen staff and ate a bowl of Brunswick stew with a slice of cornbread. Soon, customers began to arrive, and she hurried out to seat them and take their orders. There were two other waitresses as well as herself, so though they were busy, it wasn't overwhelming. And the whole crew worked together well.

The cafe filled up quickly. Before long, darkness fell, letting the twinkle lights in the courtyard and the candles on each table shine. While she was bussing a table, she felt a hand on the small of her back. She spun around to find herself pressed up close to Ryan. He leaned forward to kiss her forehead, then lingered.

"Hmm ... no lips, huh?"

She squirmed out of his grasp. "That's right. It's for the best. What are you doing here?"

"That's a nice welcome from a wife," he said with a frown.

"Fake wife," she whispered, making sure no one heard her.

"Not according to the United States Government."

She rolled her eyes. "Can I get you a table?"

"No need, I'm sitting with friends. I thought I'd come over and say hello."

"Hello."

He smirked, stepped closer until she had no escape with the kitchen wall right behind her. "Do I make you uncomfortable?"

She smiled. "Not at all, husband." Truthfully, her heart was firing at a rapid pace, and she needed to get away from him. He smelled too good. What was his cologne? It always made her knees weak. "There's going to be live music later," she said, trying to change the subject. "And dancing."

"Really? Maybe you should save me a dance then." He let his gaze fall to her lips, then spun on his heel and strode away.

She released the breath she'd held in her lungs and let the tension ease from her shoulders. She couldn't think straight when he stood so close to her. He towered over her and made her nervous. She wished he'd keep out of her space. She'd have to talk to him about her personal bubble.

* * *

By the time the live band started to play, the entire cafe was hopping. Conversations buzzed, laughter peeled through the electric atmosphere, the scents of BBQ sandwiches and margaritas combined with the smoke of the candles and the perfume of the partygoers to form an intoxicating aroma.

Matilda was run off her feet keeping the food coming and the dirty dishes going. Finally, everyone had finished their dessert and was settled around the dance floor with drinks. She leaned against the bar to catch her breath and watch the fun. Ryan caught her eye and dipped his head towards the dancers.

She laughed and undid her apron, then walked over to him. He held out one large hand and she took it. He led her to the dance floor and pulled her into his arms so quickly and gracefully it stole her breath away.

He was a good dancer. Who would've imagined? So lanky, so comfortable in his ever-present jeans and brown jacket, with his hat hair and his sun browned skin, and yet so light on his feet. He was a mixture of so many things she could barely keep it all straight in her head. Who was he really? What made him tick? She still had no idea. Yet right now, in this moment, she didn't care.

She leaned into him, letting him take over. Her feet had never glided so easily across a dance floor, she'd never felt so adept at moving. It was as if they were one, melded together with their hands and arms joined.

"Why didn't you tell me you owned a construction company?" she asked. She had to shout to be heard over the noise of the band.

He dipped his head towards her, his gaze intense. "What do you mean? I thought you knew."

"I didn't know. My first impression was that you were the handyman for the bed and breakfast."

He laughed, his eyes twinkling. "No, I own it. It's one of my investment properties. I just like doing some of the work myself. It helps me unwind at the end of a stressful day. Especially when the actual handyman is on vacation."

She shook her head slowly. "Well, that makes a lot more sense."

"Do you miss being a vet?"

She thought about it for a moment. "Yes, I do. I miss the animals. Not the stress. It can be a very emotionally taxing job. I love animals. I don't love having to see them sick and in pain all of the time or having to put them down every day."

"Will you go back to it?"

"I think so. Although in the meantime, I'm hoping to convince Rita to let me get some animals at the lake house. We have Blue, but he's so old I hardly know he's there half the time."

He grunted. "Good luck with that. Anyway, I was considering getting a dog. Maybe you could help me pick one out."

Joy surged. "I would love that. There's nothing in the world better than bringing home a little puppy, cuddling it, training it, taking care of it. It's my favourite pastime. Sugar glider joeys come close, but dogs are still number one."

"What's a sugar glider?"

"It's a tiny possum with wings."

"What on earth?" His eyes widened. "I had no idea those existed."

"They're quite literally the cutest creature in the world." She sighed. "Sometimes I foster them when they've been separated from their mother."

"Sounds interesting."

"Do you like animals?"

He shrugged. "I've never had much to do with them. We had a cat when I was a kid. I'm not big into cats."

"I can understand that, but I think you'll like having a dog."

"That house is too big and empty. I need someone to keep me company," he said in a rare moment of vulnerability.

She could see the emotion behind his eyes.

"I think that's a good idea."

He spun her around, then dipped her. She laughed out loud, her hair flying out in every direction as she went. Then, she was back in his arms again, pressed to his chest and feeling the warmth of his embrace.

She looked up into his eyes, still grinning. He was watching her closely, a smile tugging at one corner of his mouth.

"This is fun," he said.

"So fun," she agreed without breaking eye contact.

Chapter Twenty-Eight

That night, after the cafe was cleaned up and closed, Matilda drove home in the pitch darkness. The sky had clouded over, there wasn't even a hint of moon shining through. She had to use the brights to follow the lake road to the house. All she wanted to do was drink some hot chocolate and crawl into bed to sleep like the dead for as long as she was able.

But there was one issue: Rita still hadn't called her back. Hopefully, she'd find her at the house. Although she'd had to borrow the old beat-up car from behind the cafe in order to get home. Amanda had found the keys in the office and given them to her with strict instructions to be careful with the clutch.

She pulled into the driveway and climbed out of the car. Rita's truck wasn't in the drive. *Hmmm.* That meant Rita had gone somewhere and not come home, without telling Matilda or answering her phone. Matilda had taken an Uber to work, since she'd had no other option. Maybe Rita had decided to visit Julie in Athens, but why wouldn't she shoot through a text to let Matilda know?

Likely she just forgot. It was the most obvious explanation. She shouldn't get so anxious. Rita would show up tomorrow morning with a simple story about how she'd let her phone battery die or something similar, and she'd laugh at Matilda's overly anxious raft of text messages.

Before she could get to the front door, the bottom fell out of the clouds, followed by a loud crack of thunder. It scared her half to death and made her jump. She quickly opened the door and rushed inside, but not before she was soaked through. She peered outside through the large dormer windows in the back of the house at the dock. The boat was tied tightly to the moorings; it would be fine. Fat raindrops splashed into the water, sending more droplets flying. She could see them via the outdoor floodlights that'd been tripped by her movements when she came in.

It'd rained a lot lately. The ground was absolutely soaked. She'd padded through mud to get to the house. Now she kicked off her shoes at the door and then went to get a hot shower. She dried off and dressed in her most comfortable PJs, a pair of short shorts, with a long-sleeved but very low cut top that were practically see through she'd worn them so many times. But since she was here alone, it really didn't matter whether they were skimpy or not, no one else would see them.

In the kitchen, she made some hot cocoa. Then, she carried the cup to the chair by the dormer windows and sat down, her knees bent up, to watch the rain fall. It thundered against the rooftop and made her feel cosy, all snug in the house. It had turned cool when the sun set, but now that the rain was falling a little, humidity had snuck into the air. Still, she shivered, so she turned the heat up a little with the remote control.

Her phone rang, and she pressed it to her ear. "Hello?"

"Hey, it's Ryan."

"Hi, Ryan." Excitement buzzed in her gut at the sound of his voice.

"Is Rita there with you?"

"No, I'm not sure where she is, and she's still not answering her phone."

"I'm sure she's fine. But I'm watching the weather report and things could get a little dicey."

"What do you mean?" She frowned, peering out into the darkness.

"We've had so much rain lately and this hurricane might cause flash flooding around the lake and lowlands."

"Hurricane? Flooding? Does this house flood?" she asked, eyes widening.

"It does," he replied. "How did you manage to not hear about the hurricane?"

"I don't really watch the news," she sheepishly replied.

"Well, you should. You've only got one level there. If this rain keeps going, I'd recommend you put valuables up high and come on over here. We can stay on the top floor at my place, and we'll be fine. No flood has ever reached that height."

"Seriously? It could get that bad?"

"That's what they're saying."

She hesitated. "Okay, I'm going to do that now. I don't want to risk it."

"Good idea. I'll come and get you."

"Thanks."

She hung up the phone, then looked around. What was valuable? What should she put up high? Maybe she should add towels at the bottom of each door? She raced about the house getting it ready in case of flooding the best way that she could, then packed herself a small bag. Ryan let himself in and stood by the door, dripping on the entry tiles to wait for her. He wore an oversized black raincoat with a hood and heavy boots.

He took one look at her skimpy see-through pjs and grinned. "Uh, you might want to put on a little more than that. It's pretty cold out."

She glanced down and quickly covered herself with her arms. "Sorry, I forgot about that."

"No apology necessary." He laughed. "You ready?"

"I'll just change quickly."

She pulled on some sweats and covered up with a raincoat, then tugged on her hiking boots. Her backpack was waterproof, thankfully, so her things should stay dry on the walk over to his house. With one last glance around her room and anxiety bubbling in her stomach, she marched out to Ryan and the two of them splashed through the yard together.

She could already see that the lake levels were higher than usual. Both yards were sodden with large puddles gathered in places. And the rain continued to pummel them with fat, heavy drops.

Inside, she stripped off the raincoat and hung it on a peg by the door. The downstairs of his house was in a state of half-completion. The walls weren't painted, and there wasn't a stick of furniture. But tools were lying about, and she could already see that it would be an amazing living space with tall, wide bifold glass doors across the back leading out onto a massive deck that overlooked the lake.

She carried her backpack upstairs where she found soft furnishings, modern but cozy décor, and some impressive artwork hanging on the walls. His house was beautiful.

"Wow, this is great," she said in awe.

"Thanks, it's a work in progress."

"You have a good eye for design."

"It doesn't really come naturally to me, but I try."

"You've done a great job."

"Do you have your own place in Brisbane?"

He'd clearly listened and remembered what she'd told him

about where she lived. "I was renting. My lease ended before I came over here, and I put my things in storage."

"So, you're homeless?"

"I'm officially homeless, other than Rita's hospitality, of course."

"Still no word from her?"

"No, but I wondered if perhaps you had Julie's phone number? I don't know how to reach her but she might know where Rita is."

"Good idea, I'll send her a text. Here's your room." He opened a door and beckoned Matilda inside.

It was a lovely, spacious room with a queen-sized bed that was made up with a light blue comforter. There was a large chest of drawers against one wall, and a huge window looking out across the lake—or it would, if it wasn't pitch dark and raining outside. All she saw now was a blackness that made her shiver.

"Thanks, this is perfect."

"Get settled in and then you can join me for a drink if you like. Or go to bed. It's up to you."

"A drink sounds good."

They sat together in the living room, drinking whiskey (which she still wasn't sure she liked since it tasted a bit too much like cough syrup), and playing twenty-one. He kept winning, much to her dismay, since she'd never really played the game before. When she actually managed to get twenty-one in a hand, she threw her cards down in surprise with a shout, and then jumped up on her chair to dance, fists pumping.

When Ryan burst out laughing at her, she couldn't help doing the same. And they both ended up in stitches, with her leaning against his side as they laughed.

"You're a clown," he finally said, after catching his breath. "I've never seen someone dance so badly and still look so cute."

She gazed up at him, still gasping for breath. Her sides ached and her head was light. He was so handsome. She didn't know how she was supposed to resist and remain professional. She'd only recently ended a long-term relationship and had planned on staying single for a while. Besides, she didn't know how long she'd stay in this country. It didn't make any sense for her to begin something. And she wasn't a fling kind of gal.

Still, looking up at him, nestled so close to him, her only remaining thought was to wonder whether he would kiss her.

He licked his lips, his smile fading. His eyes were dark and intense. He straightened, putting a hand on either side of her face, cupping her cheeks in his palms.

"Matilda..." he whispered. "I..." Then, he shook his head, leaned in and let his lips rest lightly on hers.

His kiss stole her breath away. She reached her arms around his neck and deepened the kiss. Gently, at first, his lips searched hers. Then, her own lips parted, and he groaned softly against her, the searching becoming more urgent.

She pulled away. He blinked.

"I should go to bed," she said.

She still couldn't believe she'd had the strength to back away. But it was for the best. They should take things slow. She couldn't think when she was here with him like this. And she needed to be certain this was what she wanted. She'd fallen into a relationship with Cam years ago and coasted along when she should've walked away. She didn't want to do the same thing again, although she'd never felt *this* way before.

"You're right," he said, clearing his throat. "We need to get some space. Think things through."

"Take it slow," she added.

"Yeah, exactly."

He inhaled a deep breath. "I'll see you in the morning, then."

"Good night," she replied.

As she walked to her room, she raised her eyes skyward. "What is wrong with me?"

Chapter Twenty-Nine

When Matilda woke the next morning, she opened the drapes to peer out through sleepy eyes at the lake below. It was the colour of mud and had travelled up to the steps of Rita's house, but didn't look as though it'd gone inside. She was immediately grateful and whispered a prayer of thanks.

She dressed quickly and hurried out to the kitchen. She found Ryan frying bacon, a tea towel slung over one shoulder. His hair was mussed, and he wore a pair of sweatpants that hung low on his narrow hips. His muscled torso was tanned and lean ... and shirtless.

"It doesn't look like the water level made it up to the house," she said, sitting down on a bar stool at the kitchen counter.

He smiled at her. "Good morning. The rain has stopped too, so I think the worst is behind us."

"I'm so glad. I'd hate for Rita's house to flood. Especially when I don't even know where she is."

"She texted me back," he said. "Sorry, I didn't want to wake you, but I know you've been worried about her."

"Is she okay?"

"She's at the hospital."

"What?" Matilda stood up, her stomach clenching. "What happened?"

"She's okay." He beckoned her to sit again. "She says she's fine, anyway. Julie is with her. Apparently, the doctor wanted to run some more tests and convinced her to spend the night. And then her phone battery went dead, and she didn't have her charger. She said to apologise, she should've found a way to contact you and let you know."

Matilda breathed out a sigh of relief. "Okay. Well, thank goodness for that."

"I told her the house was safe. And that you were here with me."

"Thanks for doing that."

"You're welcome. How do you like your eggs?"

He handed her a piece of bacon and she took a bite. It burned her tongue, and she blew on it while chewing. "Hot ... hot!"

"Sorry, should've warned you."

"Um ... scrambled. But you don't have to do all of that. Really ... you've done so much already."

"Have I?" He frowned as he cracked eggs into a bowl.

"You checked on me, let me stay here, then contacted Rita for me. Plus that whole fake marriage thing. You've really gone above and beyond..."

"I am your husband, after all." He winked.

"That's true. Maybe I'm not expecting *enough* from you. Did you take out the rubbish?"

He laughed. "Do you mean the trash? I think the trash may have floated away ... so, no."

"Wow, slack." She replied with sass.

He poured the eggs into the frying pan ,and they sizzled in the bacon grease.

"Do you have plans for today?"

"I'm supposed to work at the cafe."

"Maybe we can..."

She finished chewing her bite of bacon and stood again, pushing the bar stool back. This was all too much. The guest room, the glistening chest, the tasty bacon, and the hint of future plans ... it was all so very domestic. So perfect. And yet, she felt a panic attack looming at the edges of her conscious mind. Her chest was tight, and her head spun.

"Um ... yeah, rain check?" She laughed, pointing outside. "Literally. Uh ... okay, well, thanks for the bacon. But I think I should run. I've got a lot to do today."

"What's going on?" His brow furrowed and he set down the spatula. "Why are you acting weird?"

"I'm not weird, you are." She took several steps backwards.

"I didn't say you were weird, but you're definitely acting weird. I didn't ask you to marry me ... oh wait..."

He was attempting to break the tension with humour. She recognised the strategy because she used it all the time. But it wouldn't work, not now, not when her heart rate was through the roof and her thoughts in a whirl.

She wrung her hands together. "The thing is, I just got out of this really intense relationship. And he broke up with me. I'm still recovering."

"Did you love him?"

"I thought I did, but I realise now that probably wasn't the case."

"Then, what's the problem?"

"It's so much ... we've only known each other for a couple of months. We're already married, you're making me breakfast while looking like ... that." She pointed at him. Then groaned. "It's a bit overwhelming. I'm sorry, I'm not very good at the whole intimacy thing. And I'm not sure I'm going to stick around, so does it make sense to get close to someone?"

He crossed his arms, studied her. "You're really losing it, huh?"

"No, not losing it." She wrinkled her nose. "I'm..."

"You're having a meltdown because we kissed," he replied smugly.

"Definitely not. Meltdowns are for toddlers. I'm an adult and I'm having a rational and logical..."

"Meltdown," he concluded, finishing her sentence for her.

Her eyes narrowed. "That's ... really...."

"What?"

"I'm going."

"Okay, I guess I'll see you later then."

She raced back to her room and grabbed her backpack, then headed for the door. He didn't come after her or try to stop her. Didn't say a word. She slammed the door shut behind her and trudged through the slop and mud back to Rita's house. How dare he claim she was acting childishly. He was rushing her, if anything. And she needed some time to think about what was happening between them. She'd seen their marriage as a convenience, nothing more than that. He'd given no indication that he had feelings for her, other than irritation and annoyance. And now he expected her to be ready to jump into something that might be a huge mistake. As far as she knew, he might only want a fling. And she wasn't interested in anything like that.

If he wanted to get to know her better, she'd give him that chance. But she wasn't about to jump headfirst into a minefield. Not with everything else in her entire life up in the air the way it was. She didn't know anything about her biological parents yet. Still hadn't figured out the mystery of her birth. Her mother and father were dead. Her siblings thousands of miles away in Australia. And her recently discovered aunt was in the hospital. Kissing Ryan Merritt was the very last thing she should be doing right now.

Chapter Thirty

There was a gigantic crash in the kitchen. Matilda smiled apologetically at her customers and excused herself to rush in there. Milly, the new teenaged dishwasher, stood in the centre of the tiled floor with a pile of broken plates around her. Her face was stricken, and she clearly didn't know what to do next.

Matilda hurried to help her, reaching for the dustpan and brush as she went. "Never mind. I'll sweep, you pick up the big pieces and put them in the bin."

"Oh no, I'm sorry," she said, her eyes brimming with tears. "That was a lot of plates."

"There's no point getting upset about it now," Matilda said sternly. "What's done is done." When did she start to sound like her mother? She'd slipped into the role without even realising it.

"Will Rita be angry?"

"I doubt it. I'm sure she's dropped a thousand plates in her time."

Milly bent to retrieve the larger pieces of plates that had survived the fall while Matilda got to work sweeping up the rest and dumping it into the rubbish bin.

Suddenly she heard raised voices in the dining area. With a frown, she scurried out to see what was going on. Rita was still under the weather and had gone home to rest after her time in the hospital, so Matilda was running the cafe today and was completely overwhelmed. It hadn't been too busy, but everything kept going wrong. And she'd given up attempting to seat people, instead leaving it to the waitresses.

She found Rita's cousin Cathy standing in the dining room, waving her arms about. Two men were with her, dressed in long pants and buttoned-down shirts. They were looking around the room and taking notes. Cathy's voice was raised as she explained the history of the building and the materials used in its construction.

The seated guests were watching the whole event with interest and confusion.

Matilda didn't want to be rude, but she interrupted Cathy as soon as she could get the woman's attention. "Hi, Cathy. Do you remember me, Matilda?"

Cathy glared at her. "Oh yes, the Aussie girl."

"That's right. I'm managing the cafe today. Just wondering what's going on here?" She did her best to look humble and helpful. Cathy seemed like the type to eat her whole given half the chance.

Cathy turned to face her, hands on hips. "I'm getting the cafe valued."

"Ah, okay ...why?"

Cathy's cheeks grew pink, her eyes flashed. "Because I want to. That's why. And if we're going to sell the place, I'd like to know how much I could get for it."

"Can we ... come over to the side?" Matilda asked, ushering the three of them towards the office. They squeezed into the small space, and she shut the door.

They stood like fish fingers in a line staring at her.

"That's better. Thanks—I don't think the customers need

to hear all of this. And I have questions ... like what on earth are you talking about? Who is selling?"

Cathy sighed. "This cafe belongs to me and to Rita. I'm considering my options for it—one of which is to sell. The other involves a renovation and possibly a bar. But I'm still undecided. Does that satisfy your unhelpful curiosity?"

"Here's the thing, Cathy. Rita has left me in charge today, so if you want to poke around, you're going to have to get me onside. And right now, you're failing in that quest."

Cathy eyed her as if she was a cat watching a mouse. "Don't sass me."

"No, ma'am." Matilda had learned a few things during her time in Covington. And she knew when to use the honorific.

"This cafe belonged to my father alongside Rita's father. They were brothers. They passed it on to me and her. I've never staked my claim before now, but I think it's time I did. None of which has anything at all to do with you."

Matilda smiled. "That's absolutely fine. Just make sure you come back when Rita is here so she can give you permission. But thanks for stopping by."

She watched them leave, anger forming a knot in her stomach. How dare Cathy take advantage of Rita's absence to stake an ownership claim on the cafe. This was the last thing Rita needed right now. Matilda was not going to stand idly by and let it happen. She wouldn't let Cathy steal away something so precious from a woman who'd already lost so much and who had the biggest heart of anyone she'd ever met.

Chapter Thirty-One

The candles on the cake flickered in the light breeze that filtered through the oak leaves on the trees that lined the back-yard. Helen had bought a house. It wasn't a big house—it was tiny, in fact—but it had a great backyard. And that was what really mattered, to her way of thinking.

She'd fenced the yard, put a dog in it, and now she and Julie spent most of their free time back there. Julie toddled around on her little chubby legs, so new to walking that she fell as often as not. Meanwhile, Helen did the gardening, sipped tea on the back porch, or pushed Julie on the swing. It was their happy place. And Helen didn't take it for granted.

Julie was one year old. The cake wasn't perfect. It was meant to be a pair of ballerina slippers, but one slipper had slid to the side and looked more like a pink banana. Still, no one minded. The fact that Helen and Julie had made it through the first twelve months of Julie's life was still something of a miracle. The baby had barely slept at first, had terrible reflux for a good six months, and had started walking early—which meant no rest for her mother.

But lately things had settled down. She was sleeping through the night. The reflux had abated. She was eating well. And she'd stopped running into the coffee table with her forehead since she was a little taller than the table now.

Life was good.

Finally, Helen could honestly say that she was happy. Most of the time, anyway.

The small crowd sang happy birthday. Her parents and Rita were there along with Paul's parents, siblings and a few close friends. She'd pulled away from most of their friends after Paul's death. She couldn't bear to be around them. They had such long faces, oozed pity, and wanted to avoid any and every mention of her husband. She needed to break free, start over. And so she did.

She moved to another town, not far away, but far enough to warrant another circle of acquaintances. She'd changed jobs to one that better suited being a mother. As an RN at a local aged care facility, she could work three days per week from nine-to-five and get home in time to collect Julie from daycare, have dinner together and put her to bed. She wished she could have more time at home with her, but for now, this was all they could manage. Paul's pension gave her the flexibility to stay home with Julie part of the week, and the money she needed to put a downpayment on a small home with a yard that backed onto a deeply wooded area. Sometimes there were deer in their yard. It was paradise.

They cut the cake, and Julie smooshed some into her mouth. The delight on her face at the first taste of frosting was more than worth the hours that had gone into baking it and decorating it. Helen had been up until midnight putting the finishing touches on the cake and packing the party bags with gifts and treats.

Filled with sugar, the one-year-olds scattered throughout the yard now, headed for the swing set, the sandpit, and the dog who was running away as fast as she could, tail tucked. Helen caught the dog and shoved her into the house, shutting the door behind her.

She followed Julie around the yard. The child settled in the sandpit and began scooping sand into a yellow bucket.

"She's beautiful," Rita said, coming up behind her.

"She really is."

"That hair..." Rita said. Everyone always commented on it. So much thick, dark hair. She hadn't known babies could have hair like that. It looked as though she'd had it styled at a salon. It already reached halfway down her back.

"I know. I'm not really sure what to do with it. Should I cut it? I'll have to at some stage, or she'll sit on it. And she's always getting it in her food."

"I can't relate," Rita replied with a chuckle. "I've never had hair that grew so fast or thick."

"Me either," Helen replied, tugging at her own short, thin, blonde locks.

"I wonder where she got those eyes, too." Rita frowned. "They're so brown. It's like she's looking into my soul. She grabs me by the ears and peers into my eyes and says *Rita.* I would give her anything at that moment. A pony? Do you want a pony? Aunt Rita will buy you one, little darling." She spoke the last words in a song-song voice pointed at Julie, who laughed out loud in that cheeky little bubbling laugh that was so contagious.

Helen had often thought the same thing though. She loved her daughter so much. But where did the dark brown eyes, the thick, brown hair, and the compliant personality come from? Paul had hazel eyes and light brown hair. She and her entire family were blonde with blue eyes. Maybe it was a recessive gene? She wished she'd paid more attention in biology. Was it even possible? She couldn't recall. Regardless, she was all Helen had in the world, and she was perfect. It was because of Julie that Helen had managed to keep putting one foot in front of the other after Paul was gone. If it hadn't been for her, she didn't know if she'd have been able to go on.

Chapter Thirty-Two

CURRENT DAY

Rita sat with her back to the wall, waiting. The clock above her line of vision ticked slowly. It seemed slow anyway. Slower than usual. It was funny how that worked. When you had nothing to do but wait, clocks always ticked more slowly.

The cafe was almost entirely empty. There was one woman in the back, working on a laptop and her third cappuccino. It was the after-lunch lull before the evening crowd came rushing back in on their way home from work.

Ever since her visit to the hospital, she hadn't felt well. It might have all been in her mind, but finding out that she had oesophageal cancer wasn't exactly the highlight of her fifty-eight years of living. They'd done a PET scan and hadn't found any other cancer in her body, so the oncologist was hopeful. Surgery should do the trick—that plus radiation and she'd likely make a full recovery.

How likely? Rita had asked.

The oncologist's smile had drooped a little then. "Fifty-fifty."

So ... not very likely. Not really. She'd tapped her fingers on the desk in a slow rhythm, taking it all in. She might die. Not only might she die, but there was a fifty-fifty chance she would. And when she read up about it later, the chance of death increased after five years.

Yippee!

Something to look forward to.

Just then, Julie pushed through the doorway. She had a satchel slung across her body. Her thick brown hair hung long, almost to her waist and parted in the middle. She wore glasses and her brown eyes searched the cafe until they rested on Rita's face. Then she grinned, revealing white teeth, slightly prominent in the front.

Rita stood to embrace her niece. She loved her more than anything in this world. She was so grateful for her. Tears sprang to her eyes as she squeezed tight and wouldn't let go.

"Are you okay?" Julie asked, holding onto her aunt.

"I'm fine." Rita sniffled, sat down. "Just fine. How are you?"

"I'm good. That drive gets shorter every time I do it."

"I hope you're not speeding."

Julie rolled her eyes. "I'm not speeding, worry wort." She took a seat at the table.

Rita had poured sweet tea for them both and set a pitcher in between them. The staff was under strict orders to make them each a chicken pot pie for lunch just as soon as Julie was seated.

She took a swig of tea. Julie set her satchel down on the seat beside her.

"It's so nice to see you."

"You saw me last week, at the hospital," Julie replied with a laugh.

"I know. But it's never enough."

"How are you feeling? Really?"

Rita sighed. "I could be better. Mostly, I'm anxious. The surgery is scheduled for two weeks from today."

"I'll be on spring break. I can come and take care of you."

"Would you? That would take a load off my mind."

"Of course I will." Julie reached out to hold one of Rita's hands. She squeezed it. "Don't you have someone staying with you already though?"

"Yes, Matilda is at the house. She's ... well, I've been meaning to talk to you about her. And a few other things. That's why I wanted to meet for lunch."

"Okay, I'm listening."

A waitress brought their pot pies and set them on the table. They looked delicious with steaming crunchy golden pastry on top and served with a side of rice.

"I'm starving," Julie said, picking up her fork. "What did you want to talk about?"

Rita moved her fork around on the table. "Well, firstly, it's about Matilda."

"It's a bit strange you've got her living with you. I have to say that."

"There's a reason for it. You see ... she's your cousin. I think she is. I'm not entirely sure."

"Huh?" Julie gaped. "What do you mean, my cousin?"

"I don't know exactly, honey. Just that she came into the cafe and told me she'd done a DNA test and was looking for Tyler Osbourne, her cousin. So, we talked, and I spent some time with her, and I think she's telling the truth. Anyway, I'm going to do a DNA test to see if she really is connected to me. But that's why she's staying at the house."

Worry etched Julie's features. "You let a stranger, claiming to be my cousin, move into the lake house with you? With no proof?"

"She showed me the test results," Rita objected. Although

now, hearing Julie's words, she did wonder if she'd been foolish.

"You're far too trusting, Aunt Rita." Julie ate a bite of pie.

"Maybe you're right. I'll get to the bottom of it."

"Even if she's telling the truth, how could that be? Whose kid is she?"

"That's what I don't know. You're an only child. In my family, there was just me and Helen. So unless there's another relative we don't know about..."

"Okay, well, I definitely think we should do a bit more digging on that."

"Regardless, I think you'll love her. She's such a nice girl. She's been so good to me, taking care of me and helping out around the cafe. She's Australian, I think I mentioned that."

"I'm grateful to her for that. I just worry about you," Julie said. "I'll tell you what. I'll leave my hairbrush with you, and you can get my DNA to compare with hers. I don't want to be difficult or contrary, but I care about you, and I don't want to see you taken advantage of."

"I hear you," Rita replied. "I'll get all the tests done. I don't think Matilda will mind, in fact, that's what she came here to do—to find the truth about who she is."

"Okay."

"And there's another thing." She cleared her throat. "You know I'm sick, right?"

"I know ... but we'll get through this. The doctors said we'd caught it in time."

"Maybe, we're staying positive anyway. But my cousin Cathy is causing a stink. She's going after the cafe."

"What does that mean?" Julie's brow furrowed with worry lines.

Rita explained the situation to Julie, who stopped eating and put her fork down on the table.

"So, she thinks she can just come along, all these years

later, and take half of the cafe from you? When you've worked so hard to keep it going and make it into an institution in Covington?"

Rita nodded. "That's exactly what Matilda said."

Julie huffed. "Well, that's not going to happen. I won't let it."

They ate in silence for a few minutes. Then, Rita spoke up again. "You know I'd hoped to give you the cafe someday."

Julie swallowed and reached for her tea. She drank quietly, then looked at Rita with tears in her eyes. "I'm sorry, but you know I'm studying to be a psychologist."

"I know you are. And I'm so proud of you."

"I don't love the cafe the way you do."

"So, maybe I should let it go then?" Rita mused, leaning back in her chair.

She'd grown up in this place. Watched her father develop the recipes in the old kitchen. It'd been done up several times since then, renovated, expanded, and modernised. But the bones of it remained. It was a relic of her childhood, her past. A history untold and unremembered by anyone other than her and Cathy. Her parents were gone. Her sister had died. The cousins who'd run about the cafe with her decades earlier had moved away. All but Cathy.

"You shouldn't let it go. You're acting like your sickness has already won. I can't listen to this." Julie pressed both hands to her ears, looking stricken.

Rita reached for her hands and gently moved them down. "I haven't given up. I promise."

"I can't lose you as well..." Julie's voice broke.

"You won't. I'm going to fight this thing, for your sake. I will." She'd been tempted to give up, to let go of all the things she'd been clinging to for so long. But seeing Julie's face, hearing her tortured words, she couldn't do that to her niece.

She owed it to her to do everything in her power to take this battle all the way.

"Thank you," Julie said. "I don't have anyone but you. Dad's family live so far away, and they love me, I know that. But I don't see them much. If you leave me ... I'll be all alone in the world."

"I'm not going anywhere." Rita replied with a sigh. "But I do have to think about what's best for the cafe. And for me. Maybe it'd help me to have Cathy shoulder some of the load around here."

"You do need help. But not from Cathy. You can't stand each other. You'll be far more stressed with all the conflict between you than you are now."

Rita patted Julie's hand. "You're probably right about that. But the problem is, she's also right. Her dad was part owner of this place. And truthfully, I can't say one way or the other whether she inherited a portion of it."

"How can you find out?"

"I suppose I'll have to talk to my lawyer."

"I'll do anything I can to help. I know I'm not a lawyer and I don't know much about anything, but I don't think you should give up a single piece of this cafe. Not to Cathy. Sell the whole thing if you like to someone who'll care for it. But don't give it away. Cathy doesn't have the right personality to run The Honeysuckle, and you know that. Imagine how the staff would revolt!"

Rita laughed at that. She was right. "Amanda would tip cornbread batter down Cathy's shirt and storm out on day one."

"You'd have a mass exodus," Julie continued as she giggled along with her aunt.

"A communist revolt!"

"The overthrow of tyranny!"

"It'll be gossip all over town," Julie added.

"Oh heck, I'll be on the news, won't I? Local cafe owner arrested for the stabbing death of her cousin..."

They laughed until their sides hurt. Rita couldn't remember when she'd laughed so hard. Probably not since Helen's death.

Finally, they calmed themselves, and Rita wiped the tears from her eyes with a napkin. She inhaled a deep, cleansing breath. "You're absolutely right. You've got so much wisdom for your age, honey. I couldn't work with Cathy. It'd be a bloodbath."

"So, we'll figure out something else."

"Yes, we'll have to. Because I'm getting too tired to manage everything myself. And with treatments..."

"I wish I could do something to help you," Julie replied with a sympathetic look.

"At least Matilda is here. She's been such a help to me already. And I'm sure she wouldn't mind taking on a little more responsibility."

"If you think you can trust her..."

"I do. But I'll keep you updated on that."

Rita understood her niece's reluctance to embrace this stranger from the other side of the world. But there was something about Matilda that Rita immediately liked. Not to mention the fact that she looked and behaved so much like Helen. Even the way she smiled reminded Rita of her sister. She didn't want to say anything to Julie about it, wasn't sure how her niece would take it. It'd always been a sore spot for her that she and Helen were nothing alike. And she might not take kindly to finding a stranger with more of a family resemblance than she had.

Chapter Thirty-Three

The clean up after the hurricane involved a lot of sweeping, scraping, and tramping about in knee-high gum boots. Thankfully the brunt of the storm had burned itself out over the ocean and the tip of Florida, and Jackson Lake had mostly had rain with some gusts of wind. The damage was minimal, although there were a few tree branches and a lot of twigs and leaves scattered around the lake.

Matilda had spent the morning cleaning up Rita's backyard with Ryan's help. Rita wanted to join in, but they both insisted she stay indoors and provide drinks and snacks instead. Which she did with enthusiasm, bringing out freshly squeezed lemonade and blackberry muffins when Ryan and Matilda were taking a break.

After the clean-up, Matilda had taken a shower and then carried the envelopes containing her own DNA results, along with hair samples from Julie and a saliva sample from Rita, into town to mail. She was nervous but excited at the prospect of finally discovering whether or not she was connected to Rita and Julie. Although she was fairly certain the results would prove she was, given that she'd already found a connection to Tyler, Rita's son.

But Julie and Rita was both still skeptical. Rita believed her, she was certain of that. But she didn't see how the connection was possible, and they all hoped that these tests would be the ultimate explanation they were all searching for. Matilda still hadn't met Julie. The girl seemed to be adept at avoiding her, whether intentionally or not, she couldn't say yet. But Rita assured her it was simply a matter of being busy and nothing more than that.

When she made it home, it was lunchtime, and she was ravenous. She ate a buffalo chicken salad—leftovers from dinner the previous evening—and then another blackberry muffin along with two large glasses of unsweetened tea. She had consumed far more sugar than usual and had gained several kilograms since she arrived. She'd have to slow down if she was going to stay much longer. So she'd taken to drinking her tea unsweetened. It wasn't the same.

There was a knock at the door just as she was rinsing off her plate to put in the dishwasher. She went to answer it, and found Ryan waiting, leaned against the door frame. He grinned at her, his smile intoxicating, his athletic frame casting a shadow into the house.

"Hey, I'm going to pick out a puppy. You wanna come?"

"Right now?"

"Yeah, right now."

She grinned back at him. "Yes, please!"

They drove about an hour to the pound. The depressing single-story grey building, surrounded by tall wire fences, was down a long road in the countryside.

"What kind of dog do you want?" she asked.

He parked the truck in one of the empty spaces in the large, rectangular parking lot. "Something I can take to work with me. Keep me company driving. That kind of thing."

"Big or small?"

"I prefer bigger dogs. Not huge, but something medium-sized maybe."

"Active or lazy?"

"I'll take it running with me every day, so pretty active, I guess."

"Well, let's see what they have."

"I called earlier. They had a litter of mixed breed Australian shepherds come in. I thought you might like the idea of another Aussie in the neighbourhood."

"You're hilarious," she said, snidely, although secretly, she couldn't help thinking that it was actually pretty sweet of him. And he'd obviously been thinking of her, which made her warm inside.

The litter of puppies was adorable. There were around a dozen of them, although it was hard to count since they never stopped moving. They were so fluffy it was impossible to tell how big they were, as most of them appeared to be fur. She guessed they were at least eight weeks old, but not much more than that.

They certainly fit all his requirements: medium-sized, intelligent, active and a great companion. There was no information about what they were mixed with, but she guessed perhaps Labrador since a few of the puppies had short, black hair and a sweet Labrador-shaped face.

The two of them sat in the cage with the puppies. The dogs crawled and jumped all over them, yipping with delight and chewing on various parts of them. Ryan's face had a softness and light to it that wasn't usually there. He was enthralled with the little creatures and spoke in a soft, high-pitched voice that would've made Matilda stifle a laugh if she wasn't doing exactly the same thing.

In the end, he selected one of the big, fluffy puppies. He

held it up to stare it in the eyes. Its eyes were small and black, and it tried to lick his nose.

He laughed and said, "This is the one."

He'd brought a box with him for the male Labrador puppy to travel home in. It whined the entire way, so Matilda did her best to comfort and distract him. Ryan decided to call him Ozzie because he said he wanted to remind her of home.

Back at the lake, Matilda carried the puppy inside the house. He was perfect. So cute and cuddly and very happy to be held. As soon as she put him down on the floor in the kitchen, he pranced towards her, lifting his paws playfully high. She and Ryan sat on the floor across from one another, and Ozzie kept dancing back and forth between them, his little tail wagging his whole body with joy.

It didn't take long for him to tire out. He was soon sleeping on a small blanket Ryan had fetched from the linen closet.

Ryan walked Matilda out as the sun was setting over the lake which lay black in the shadows of the surrounding hills.

"Thanks for helping me with that," he said. "I think he's going to be a good dog."

"The best," she replied. "And you're welcome."

He reached for her hand and pulled her back to him, so that she was pressed against his body, their hands now entwined. He looked down at her, his expression unreadable in the failing light. Her breathing grew ragged.

"Ryan..."

"I know you're not ready, but I want you to understand, I am. I never told you about my past because I didn't want to open up. I was married before. It didn't last long, only four years. But I was devastated when it ended. We were both too young, she didn't want to stay and make it work. We fought all the time. One day, she just left. I've never really let someone back into my heart since."

"I'm sorry…" was all she could think to say even as her soul ached for his pain.

"It's complicated, I get it. But for me, this isn't just another connection—one of many. It's not something I've ever felt before. I was obsessed with my wife because we were teenagers when we fell in love. But this is different. This is a mature respect, desire … heck, I just like you. I like being with you, spending time with you, talking to you. I can't wait to see you when you're not around. I look forward to you pulling that dang truck into the driveway." He laughed softly. "Am I completely off track here?"

She took a step backwards, released his hands. "You're not off track. I just need time."

His face clouded over, and he crossed his arms, scowling. "Time, huh? Okay, sure. You take your time. But for my part, I believe when you know, you know. So, you can have time, but I think you've already given me your answer." Then he spun around and stalked back into the house.

Matilda watched him go with a pain in her gut that grew and traveled up to her chest. Why did she say that? Why didn't she give him a chance? Something was holding her back. Something she didn't understand. But she hadn't been able to say what he wanted to hear, to be who he needed her to be. There were still so many things up in the air. She felt like the ground was shifting beneath her, and she could fall at any time. She couldn't give her heart away now. Not yet. Not until everything in her life made sense again.

Chapter Thirty-Four

TWENTY-THREE YEARS AGO

Helen pushed the pram into the Honeysuckle Cafe. The freshly painted dining area looked sparkling clean and bright. Her father and sister had spent the entire week painting the cafe, inside and out, and using bright colours against white trim. The dining area was blue and green. When she'd heard that, she'd wondered if it would work, but walking into the space ...she loved it. The honeysuckle vine out front was in full bloom, and there were snippets of the vine hanging in pots from the ceiling or stashed on top of bar stools all over the cafe. The greenery perfectly complimented the bright paint.

"This looks great, Rita," she said, pulling the pram up to park beside her favourite table at the window overlooking the square.

"You think?" Rita had a streak of white paint down one side of her face.

"It's perfect."

"Thanks." Rita kissed her cheek in welcome and then they

sat together at the table. A waitress brought them a pitcher of sweet tea and two glasses and took their order.

Rita peered into the pram with a look of pride and love on her face. "She's so sweet."

"Especially when she's sleeping," Helen added in a sugary voice.

They both laughed.

Rita added. "Yes, she's an angel when she's asleep. It makes me just want to kiss those chubby little cheeks."

"Don't you dare. You'll wake her up," Helen threatened.

"Yes, ma'am." Rita offered a mock salute.

Dad and Uncle Bill walked into the cafe. Dad shut and locked the door behind him. It wasn't time to open up yet, and the place still smelled a bit like paint.

"It doesn't matter, Bill," Dad said, obviously irritated.

Bill frowned. "It matters because I say it does. I've got just as much of a right..."

"You haven't been around for months. You hardly ever come into the cafe and work. And if I say the accounting software we use is fine and we don't need to spend thousands of dollars on something new, including a new PC to run it, then the conversation is over." Dad slapped his hands together.

Bill's face grew red. "You always want to have things your way."

"Not always, but this time, yes."

"This is my cafe too."

Dad hesitated, his voice grew calm. "Not anymore, Bill."

"What? What are you talking about? Y'all can't just take it from me."

The two of them disappeared into the office and shut the door behind them. The women couldn't hear them any longer, just their muffled voices raised in anger.

Helen exchanged a look with Rita. "What was that about?"

"I don't know. But I've never seen Dad get so angry."

Their father was always calm and had a smile on his face. It made Helen nervous to hear him raise his voice because it was so unusual.

Cathy traipsed into the cafe, using her key to gain entry. She wore a bright red pantsuit which showed off her tan, and her bangs were hairsprayed high above her forehead into a wave shape. She smacked gum as she chewed and leaned against the wall, one foot propped.

"What's up, leeches?"

"Nice," Rita said, with a shake of her head.

Cathy grinned. "I'm trying not to swear. It's not ladylike, apparently. Gareth doesn't like it. So I have to come up with new names for y'all."

Her new boyfriend sounded like a real winner from what Helen had heard. Although she didn't like to judge, Cathy made that very difficult at times.

She seemed to notice the pram for the first time and leaned down to look beneath the hood where Julie was sleeping. Her brow furrowed and face hardened. "Hmmm ... doesn't look much like you, does she? She twirled her blonde hair with a finger. "Hasn't got the family locks. And that skin—pretty fair for an Osbourne, I'd say."

"Mind your own business, Cathy," Helen said with a sigh. "I don't really care what you think."

"Yeah, shut up, Cathy," Rita added. "She's beautiful and you're jealous."

Cathy laughed. "Jealous? Hardly. Gareth's about to propose and then we'll be popping out babies. You should get a DNA test for her though. Doesn't look like either one of you."

After she left, Helen met Rita's gaze with worry bubbling in her gut.

"What's wrong? Don't let her get to you. You know what she's like," Rita said.

"I know, it's just that ... she's not the first person to say something. I mean, she's the first to be so rude about it, but I've had that comment from dozens of people over the past eighteen months."

"Dozens?" Rita arched an eyebrow. "People are nosy and obnoxious. Ignore them."

"But what if she's right? What if they all are? I mean, she doesn't look like me or Paul."

"So? That doesn't mean anything. Babies come out however they come out. I was right there with you when she was born. I swear it's the same baby. I know she went to the special care nursery, but I got a good look at her."

"Are you certain?" Helen asked, feeling resolve build within her.

Rita chewed on her lower lip for a few moments, her gaze drifting from Julie's face to Helen's and back again. "Not certain..."

"Oh no!" Helen threw both hands over her face. "What if she was accidentally switched in the hospital or something awful like that?"

"It seems pretty unlikely," Rita replied.

"But it does happen."

"There's a simple way to find out, I guess." Rita inhaled a quick breath. "You just have to get her tested."

Chapter Thirty-Five

CURRENT DAY

The weeks passed by, and Matilda fell into a routine. She liked to sleep, take a jog around the lake, then head into the cafe for work. She often worked the lunch and dinner shifts, which meant she got to bed later than she normally would. She'd gone from being an early bird to a night owl, which seemed a lateral ornithological move but meant she felt a bit lacklustre.

Winter was well and truly over now, and spring had arrived with a vengeance. Yellow pollen lay on every surface like a thick hay fever inducing blanket. Matilda had a perpetual sniffle and itchy eyes. The arrival of the humidity only made it all worse. She sat in the truck on the way to the cafe alone that morning. Rita was taking the day off, something she'd done increasingly over the past few weeks. Her surgery had been postponed due to issues with her heart, and she was feeling uncomfortable.

The traffic on the way to the cafe was always heavy. But this morning, it was at a standstill. They were about forty miles outside of the city, but Atlanta was a sprawling metropolis, and its traffic density impacted the lifestyles of people for miles in every direction. One reason being that there appeared to be very little in the way of public transportation, and even the bus and train lines that existed weren't used by many of the city's occupants. The result was a glut of six million people all heading out onto the roads at the same time and going in the same direction for the entire morning, then after lunch, they turned around and headed back together all at once.

She was grateful she didn't have to commute into Atlanta each day, but today was bad enough to make her grit her teeth in frustration. It was as if the road had been cut up ahead, no one was moving an inch. And she sat in that traffic for at least an hour, not moving, until finally the cars in front of her crawled forwards. When she passed the minor accident, the cars had been moved onto the right shoulder of the road. And the steady stream of vehicles moving by were rubbernecking so badly that it took another fifteen minutes just to creep past them.

Finally, she arrived at the cafe, but later than she'd intended. She had to run in order to catch up on getting the tables ready for the lunch crowd. She stopped in the office to check on the supplies and invoices before they opened and found a letter addressed to her. She often got her mail sent to the cafe since it was easy for her to keep track of it there, especially if she decided one day to get her own apartment. It was something she'd been considering more lately, although Rita still needed her around while she was going through treatment.

She sat in the swivel chair behind Rita's desk and opened the envelope with one finger. It was the results from the DNA comparison she, Rita, and Julie had sent to the lab. She'd slipped her sister Stella's DNA profile into the packet at the last moment on a hunch. And now she wondered if she'd done the right thing—she hadn't even asked Stella for permission. Her heart rate accelerated as her gaze skimmed over the words on the page. She glanced down at the graph below the text and saw something that made her stomach drop.

No familial connection between her and Julie.

There was no familial connection between Rita and Julie.

But Rita was indeed her aunt.

And Stella and Julie were sisters.

She stared at the results, her mind blank. It was overwhelming. Too much information. She couldn't take it all in.

She pulled her phone out of her jeans pocket and called Stella. It was late at night in Australia, but Stella would probably still be awake. She was pregnant again and had nausea induced insomnia like she had for the first trimester of her first pregnancy.

Matilda really needed to talk to her.

"Hello?" Stella sounded sleepy.

"I'm sorry, did I wake you?"

"No, I'm awake. I'm trying to get to sleep, but I keep going over my to-do list, then running to bathroom in case I throw up. Nothing yet, but it's driving me crazy. Sean is snoring too, so I've got no chance of falling to sleep."

"That's awful, you poor thing. I wish I could give you a hug."

"I'll survive. How are you?"

"I'm okay. I'm at the cafe about to start my shift. But I need to talk to you about something..."

"Before you dive into all that, can I tell you my news?"

Matilda hesitated. "Okay ... I don't have a lot of time."

"You'll want to hear this. Remember we went to see Auntie Flora? And she told us that she saw you being born?"

"How can I forget?" Matilda rubbed her hand over her forehead.

"Well, I called to check on her yesterday and she said something about how Mum and Dad had such a hard time getting pregnant with you—she called it secondary infertility—and they had to travel the States to get a round of IVF treatment done."

"What?" Matilda sat up straight, her heart pounding.

"Yeah, I thought you might find that interesting."

"I was an IVF baby?"

"Yep. They stayed there for months apparently. The clinic in Georgia was one of the best in the world. And they'd already tried everything back home. I do vaguely remember Grandma and Grandpa used to drive us to school, but we were all so little, it'd slipped my mind."

"And when they came back, Mum was pregnant with me?"

"Yep."

"I've just found out that you and Julie are sisters," Matilda said.

This time it was Stella's turn to be dumbfounded. "Who's Julie again?"

"She's Rita's niece. Rita's sister Helen's daughter."

"We're sisters?"

"That's right. And I'm Rita's niece, but no relation to Julie."

"This is all so complicated," Stella said with a groan.

"Tell me about it. I need to talk to Rita. I've got to go."

* * *

The shift at the cafe lasted as long as Methuselah. She thought it would never end. Finally, Matilda jumped in the truck and screeched out of the parking lot to head for the lake house. The after-school traffic was an absolute disaster, and she sat in the truck, chewing her fingernails, her stomach twisted into knots, while she waited impatiently to get through a four-way stop by the local school.

She needed to have this conversation with Rita in person. It wasn't the kind of thing you could talk about over the phone. She drummed her fingers on the steering wheel, then when the traffic eased up, she hit the accelerator, the truck's V6 engine grumbling to life.

By the time she reached the lake house, she was sweating, despite having the air conditioning on blast. She really should convince Rita to get the truck serviced. She hurried into the house, casting her purse aside on the hall table, and found Rita in the kitchen frying chicken.

"There you are," Rita said, with a wide smile. "I'm making fried chicken and biscuits. Do you think we need gravy? Or should I do something healthy for a side, like a salad or baked beans?"

Matilda sat on a bar stool and leaned her elbows on the counter. She felt tired. Bone tired. This wasn't a conversation she was looking forward to having. But she needed to say the words, to get to the truth. To know for certain that she wasn't crazy. That all her life, she'd been different for a reason.

"I like salad, I think that would be nice."

"Great idea, we need more greens around here. Oh, and Julie's coming to visit this weekend. Isn't that great? I convinced her it's time for her to come home. Plus, it's spring break."

"Perfect, I'm so looking forward to meeting her," Matilda said. It was high time she and Julie met and had a discussion face-to-face.

"She's excited about it too. This is going to be so great. I'm gonna make some ribs and potato salad. Maybe we should invite Ryan too, since he is your husband, after all." Rita peered at Matilda over the top of her glasses.

Matilda huffed. "You know why we did that. Don't make it weird."

"Me? Make it weird? Y'all set sail with that ship long ago."

"I need to talk to you about something," Matilda replied suddenly. She wasn't sure how Rita would take the news. But surely, she suspected something like this. They'd been talking the situation over for months, trying to figure it out. But there was still one piece of the puzzle missing. And Matilda needed to hear it from Rita's lips.

"Okay, shoot. Should I sit down for this?"

"I think that would be wise."

Rita arched an eyebrow, then switched off the stove. She lumbered into the lounge room and sat with a grunt. "My feet are killing me."

"You're supposed to be taking better care of yourself. Getting some rest. Your surgery is coming up."

"I know. Problem is, I can't sleep much at the moment. I'm so uncomfortable all of the time, and I've got the worse reflux."

Matilda sat in an armchair across from her. She inhaled a deep breath and explained what she'd discovered to Rita whose face grew more and more pale the longer she spoke. Finally, she finished her monologue and waited for Rita's response.

Rita nodded slowly, taking it all in. "I thought it would be something like that. It's been on my mind a lot lately. You know, I always knew it could be an issue. Ever since Julie was born, people always said she didn't look anything like her momma or her daddy. But they said it innocently, you know. Just the way people do. It didn't mean anything. Or at least, I didn't think so. But then you showed up and it made me think."

"Do you know if Helen ever had IVF?"

"Oh yes, she surely did."

Matilda gasped and leaned back in her chair. "Well, that settles it then. There was a mix-up at the IVF clinic. I have to confirm they attended the same one, but that's the only logical explanation. Wouldn't you agree?"

"It does seem that way, honey. The only thing is, I'm worried how Julie will take it. She doesn't know about any of this. I've told her a little about you visiting and looking for your family, that you think we're connected somehow. But this will be a blow to her, there's no getting around that. She loved her momma so well. And you say your parents are gone?"

"Both died over the past five years, I'm afraid."

"So neither one of you got to meet your folks."

Matilda's heart clenched. "No, that's true. Although I'm very grateful to have met you."

Rita reached out a hand and squeezed Matilda's. "Me too, honey. Me too."

* * *

The next day, Matilda rose early and drove to the immigration office downtown. She stood in line forever with a million other folks who wanted answers. Finally, her number was called.

She soon discovered that she could apply for a green card given her parents were US citizens, and she didn't need to be married to get the visa. She requested they make the changes to her application on the spot. She would be a green card holder within six months, they assured her, if all the supporting paperwork was supplied by the deadline.

As she drove home, she thought about Ryan and how he'd feel about that. Likely he'd be relieved to finally be rid of her after the way she'd left things with him. So, she resolved to tell him the next time she saw him. She wouldn't make a big deal of it. It wasn't something either of them should spend any time worrying about. They were never really married, after all. They could get an annulment, forget about their fake marriage and move on with their lives. It wouldn't impact them in any way. So, why did the thought of telling him put a stone in the pit of her gut?

Chapter Thirty-Six

TWENTY-THREE YEARS AGO

Helen realised too late that she shouldn't have done it. She shouldn't have gotten the test to determine who Julie's real parents were because she hadn't believed it would work out this way. She honestly hadn't. She'd thought it would put her mind at ease, not tear her entire world apart.

She sat on the bed, a pillow squeezed to her chest, and cried. She cried until the pillow was soaked, and there were no more tears left to cry. What to do now?

The letter from the IVF facility lay on the comforter beside her.

We're sorry to inform you...

Her child was in Australia. How was that possible? The other side of the world. A little girl. The parents who were raising her had called her Matilda. They'd been informed of the mishap as well and were currently no doubt processing the information just as she was. She couldn't help feeling sorry for them yet hating them a little at the same time. They were raising *her* child. They'd been raising her child for two long years. And she'd been raising theirs.

As soon as she thought of Julie, she leapt to her feet and tip-toed across the hallway to Julie's bedroom. The toddler was asleep with her arms and legs flung out like a star, covers strewn across the end of the bed and pooled on the floor. As usual. She often wondered how such a small creature could wreak such havoc on her bed each night. But laying there, she looked like an angel, with her long brown hair in braids on either side of her head, and her big eyes finally shut for the night after a long day of relentless questions.

> Why do I brush my teeth?
> Why is the toothpaste so bitey?
> Do you use toothpaste?
> If the sky is so big, why are stars so small?
> How do you know the stars are big?

And on and on. She was a precocious two-year-old with an extraordinary vocabulary. And the moment she was able to form sentences, the questions started and didn't stop until her eyes were shut.

Helen stared down at her, more tears forming and blurring her vision. Her throat ached and she wanted to groan, but didn't dare in case she woke the baby. The last thing she needed was for Julie to see her sobbing her eyes out, she'd want to know why and then what could Helen say to comfort her?

She couldn't tell anyone this. Definitely not Julie. And not her family either. It would change the way they all thought about her. She wanted so badly to have her child back, to be able to raise her and love her the way she'd always dreamed. But that would mean giving Julie to strangers on the other side of the world and never seeing her again. She couldn't do that. Couldn't give up her baby.

It was a no-win situation. There was no good solution. If they did switch toddlers, it would traumatise both children for life. Perhaps the other couple were good parents. Perhaps Matilda was happy. She hoped so. If she could find out what they were like, reassure herself that Matilda was in good hands, maybe she could let it go. Maybe she and Julie could go back to their lives and pretend none of this had happened, that it was all a bad dream. But she knew deep down that wasn't possible. Her life was changed forever. It would never be the same.

After she'd watched Julie sleep for what seemed like hours, she padded to the office and sat down at the computer. The couple in Australia had allowed the IVF clinic to share their phone number with her. She picked up the phone and dialled.

Chapter Thirty-Seven

CURRENT DAY

Matilda helped Rita to cook the next day in preparation for Julie's arrival. They'd invited Ryan to dinner, but Julie would get there first, giving them a chance to talk to her before he came over and joined them. And Matilda was nervous.

Her stomach was in knots. What if Julie was angry? What if she blamed Matilda? Hated her forever?

She shook smoked paprika over the bowl of potato salad and then leaned over the slow cooker to inhale the scent of slow-cooked spareribs in BBQ seasoning.

"This is going to be delicious, I can just tell," Matilda said, eyes gleaming.

Rita squeezed her arm lovingly. "Honey, can I just tell you again how glad I am that you came into my life? I never really had the chance to tell you this before, but the first moment I saw you in the cafe, I was shaken up by how much you resembled my sister. It was as if I'd stepped back in time and Helen was there in the cafe with me. I had to gather my senses before I could speak to you." She laughed. "And now I know why. It all makes sense. Plus, I get to have two nieces. What could be better than that?"

"I feel the same way," Matilda said, a lump growing in her throat. "I've lost my parents but now I have a brand-new aunt." She embraced Rita.

They set the table together, and by the time Julie arrived, everything was ready. There were racks of slow-cooked pork ribs, finished on the grill and doused in a sweet and sticky BBQ sauce. Along with it, there was freshly made coleslaw, corn on the cob swimming in butter and topped with salt, baked beans simmered all day on a low heat with slices of bacon and brown sugar, potato salad sprinkled with paprika, and a freshly tossed green salad.

"This looks delicious. I can't wait to try it all."

"Ribs are a southern delicacy. And the trick is to just dive in, get them all over yourself. We have paper towels at the ready." Rita laughed as she set the paper towel dispenser on the table.

"Looks good. We don't eat a lot of ribs in Australia. I wouldn't even know where to start with cooking them."

"They're pretty easy really, if you have a slow cooker."

"Noted. I'll have to get the recipe from you."

Julie walked in then, embracing Rita immediately. She turned to face Matilda with a shocked expression. She didn't speak for a few moments, then looked at her aunt.

"Is this...?"

"This is Matilda. I've told you about her. She's from Australia."

Her manners kicked in, and Julie did her best to be friendly, but Matilda could tell she was shocked by the resemblance to the woman who'd raised her as her mother. But she didn't say a word about it.

Rita and Julie sat down to eat. Matilda filled everyone's glass with sweet tea and topped each with a lime wedge. Then, she sat as well. As they ate, Rita and Matilda filled Julie in on what they'd discovered. Julie listened intently, her eyes widening with every new revelation. Finally, she stopped eating and set down her fork, her eyes brimming with tears.

"I can't believe it ... but at the same time it all makes so much sense. Mom should've told me. I would've understood."

"We can't blame her for that, she may not have known anything was up."

"We spoke about it occasionally," Rita said quietly, "We knew Julie didn't resemble anyone in the family, but we honestly believed it didn't mean anything. She mentioned an idea, once, of maybe following up with it just to set her own mind at ease. But I don't know what came of that, if anything. She never said a word more to me about it. And she told me everything. We were as close as two sisters can be."

"So ... what now?" Julie asked, glancing back and forth between the two of them.

Her hands were clenched in front of her, elbows pressed against the table, knuckles white.

"Honestly ... I have no idea," Matilda said with a shrug. "I came here to discover the truth, and I've done that. My goal now is to get to know you all, and I hope you feel the same way. I don't want to overstep. If you're not up for a relationship, that's fine."

"What about my ... I mean your ... parents?" Julie asked, her eyes bright.

"I'm afraid they've both passed. My Dad died recently, that's why I started this journey. I'm really sorry."

Julie nodded. "I wish I could've known them, but there's nothing we can do about that now."

"One thing I probably should've mentioned," Matilda said. "You have a sister and two brothers."

"Really?" Julie's eyes filled with tears. She shook her head to try to hide them.

"Yep. My sister, Stella, is amazing. You're going to love her. And my brothers are pretty great too. One is a doctor, and the other is a PE teacher. They're both married and have children."

"Wow, a whole big family. Sounds like you were lucky."

Matilda felt the depth and truth of that statement. It hit her in the chest like a mallet. All this time she'd been worried about finding the truth for herself, secure in the knowledge that no matter what she discovered, the love she and her family shared would never change. She hadn't considered how much Julie had missed. How hard her life had been, raised without a father, by a mother who died young, and with no siblings. That should've been Matilda's life.

"They're your family too," she said, her throat choking with emotion. "They're going to be so excited to meet you. And you look so much like my sister, it's a little scary to be honest." She laughed.

"I can't wait to meet them."

Chapter Thirty-Eight

The cafe wasn't busy the next morning, which gave Matilda a chance to do some cleaning and tidying of the pantry. Rita found her there, seated on a step ladder with cans and packets of food lying around her in piles.

"This is fantastic," Rita said, clapping her hands together with glee. "This pantry has needed a thorough clean out for months. Thank you for doing this."

"You're welcome. I love to organise things. It's kind of a superpower."

"It's a blessing, for sure."

"What are you doing today?"

"I have some follow-up tests at the hospital."

"That must be tiring for you. So many tests."

Rita nodded. "I'm ready for this surgery. I can tell you that. Just as soon as my cardiologist gives them the go-ahead, we'll book it in. Hopefully, I'll start to feel better after the surgery and can get my life back."

"You've been keeping up with everything pretty well, considering. You're an inspiration."

Rita crossed her eyes. "I'm sure you're exaggerating."

They both laughed.

"Hey, I wanted to talk to you about the issue with the cafe and Cathy's claim on the ownership. I've showed the paperwork to my lawyer, and she thinks I have a case. That Cathy's father abandoned the business as an active and equal partner and that legally the ownership then defaulted to my father. It's not airtight, but it's something. We're going to argue for it in court. But the problem is, I really do need help with the place. Julie can't do much, she's in school and she'll be busy with her career when she graduates. The only other person I could ask for help is Cathy. But you know what she's like." Rita rolled her eyes. "So, since you're now one of my closest relatives and you seem to enjoy working here, I wondered if you might take on a little more responsibility? And if you plan to stay a while?"

Matilda offered her a wide grin. "I would love to stay a while and help you out. The cafe is great, I'm having such a good time working here. I was stressed out in my job back at home. I needed a break. And this has been the perfect change for me. I'm actually happy and relaxed. I feel good for the first time in a long time. My anxiety is gone. I enjoy interacting with the customers. And I feel a real connection to this place —there's something special about it. Besides, the food is amazing."

"I know you can't commit forever … but it could be just the argument we need in court to bolster my ownership claim —that you're a part of the business."

"Great, I hope it helps."

"I do too."

There was a knock on the pantry door, and one of the kitchen staff let them know that Ryan was waiting outside in the courtyard to speak with Matilda. She excused herself and strode through the cafe to look for him. What did he want? She was embarrassed by how she'd behaved the last time she saw him, and her heart began to race as she considered what he might say.

He could be angry. She wouldn't blame him at all if he was. She'd thought through their interaction a thousand times since then, and every single time, she wished she'd done things differently. Still, she didn't know how she felt or what she wanted. Things were resolved now with her family—she'd uncovered the truth and felt much more settled. Maybe the timing was right. Although he'd probably moved on already. Men as good-looking as Ryan didn't wait around for a woman's mind to change.

He stood in the courtyard, hands in his pockets, staring at the honeysuckle vine which was in full bloom. The white flowers seemed to reach out for him, buttressed by thick green leaves as it climbed around the arch over the doorway and onto the timber pergola that framed the courtyard. As soon as she stepped outside, the sweet, heady aroma filled her nostrils.

"Hi," she said, shoving her hands into her jeans pockets to subconsciously match his energy.

Ryan stepped closer. "I had to come and see you. I've been meaning to catch you at home, but we both seem to be coming and going at different times."

"I've been busy with the cafe and helping Rita..."

"Me too—with work." He sighed. "I know you say you need time and I was upset about that. But I understand. My breakup was years ago. It took me a long time to recover. I can't expect you to be in the same place as me. That wasn't fair of me."

She wasn't sure what to say. Her heart ached for him. She wanted nothing more than to give in. To let the flowing river of his words carry her away. But something held her back.

"I'm glad you came to see me."

He offered her a hesitant smile. "Would you have dinner with me tonight?"

"That would be lovely."

"Great." His smile widened. "I'll pick you up around seven."

"I'll have to ask for the evening off, but I'm sure Rita won't mind."

The sound of yelling drifted through the shut glass doors. Matilda frowned and glanced through the doors, back into the cafe. She saw Cathy, waving her arms around wildly, her voice booming.

"Excuse me," Matilda said. "I have to help Rita with something."

"I'll see you tonight," Ryan said before ducking out the back gate and into the parking lot.

She opened the glass doors and stepped inside, careful to shut the doors again behind her. It would shield the neighbours from the ruckus going on inside the cafe since Cathy appeared to be having what looked like a total meltdown in the middle of the dining area. Matilda was grateful there were only two customers—both watched with shocked expressions on their faces.

"I'm so sorry," Matilda whispered to them as she went by. "I'll get you some cake. On the house."

Rita stood her ground in front of Cathy, arms patiently folded over her chest. Her face was stoic, her stance confident.

"You can't take this away from me. This cafe is as much my heritage as it is yours!" Cathy shouted, her face red. She flicked the end of the green silk scarf that was tied around her bouffant behind her shoulder to emphasise her point.

Rita's voice was steady. "You wanted to take this to court, not me, Cathy. But if you do, we'll fight back. You know our fathers had a falling out. And because of it, your dad walked away from the business. We don't know exactly what happened. None of us can say for sure what all the details were, and my dad certainly didn't talk about it with any of us.

But nevertheless, it occurred, and we've all got to live with that."

Cathy huffed, red-faced, as though her voice had been stolen.

"When your dad walked away, he gave up any claim he had to the place. According to the law. He didn't have a financial stake in the business, my dad was the one who put up the capital to start the place. They didn't have a formal partnership agreement; it was a handshake one. There's no evidence that you and your family line has any connection to the cafe. I'm sorry if that's not what you want to hear, but it's the truth."

Matilda hurried to the kitchen to get the slices of cake and carried them back to the table. By the time she was done, Cathy had stormed out of the cafe in a fit of anger. Rita turned towards her office, her face thunderous. Matilda met her there.

"Everything okay?"

"Just peachy."

"Well ... good." Matilda's phone rang. She ducked back into the courtyard to answer it. "Hello?"

"Hey, it's Stella. Is this a bad time?"

"This is a great time. I've missed you so much."

"I've missed you too. Are you coming home yet?"

"Not yet. I have news though..."

They talked about Julie and how she'd reacted to the news of her heritage.

Finally, Stella said. "I can't believe this has happened. When you first went over there, I thought you were crazy. That there was just some mishap that'd happened, and it would all work itself out. I never imagined we'd find out you were swapped with another family's baby. And it just makes me so sad."

"Don't be said," Matilda said with resolve. "I'm not. I have a whole new family to enjoy, and I still have you, right?"

"Of course you do. Nothing's ever going to change that."

"And now you have another sister as well. What could be better than gaining a new sister? I'm a little bit jealous, honestly."

Stella laughed through her tears. "You have a point. I'm sure I'll be happy about it all eventually. But for now, I just feel emotionally wrecked. I suppose I should hang up and call Todd and Bryce. I haven't told them anything yet. They're going to be flabbergasted."

"Thanks for doing that. I'd rather not call everyone individually since it's an emotional rollercoaster ride for me at the moment."

"I understand that. It's a lot for you to take in. But as you've already said, it doesn't really change anything. We're still family and we always have each other."

"I hope you'll also understand me wanting to stay for a while longer?"

Stella sniffled. "I wish you'd come home, but I get it. It makes sense you'd want to spend some time with your aunt, cousins, and everyone. Hopefully, I get to meet them all someday."

"Julie's already talking about taking a trip Down Under. She's very cute about it all, actually. I'll send you a photo. The family resemblance is uncanny. Oh and by the way, I got married."

Stella didn't speak for a moment. Then she shouted. "What? What do you mean you got married?"

After a heated conversation in which Stella accused her of being thoughtless and selfish, Matilda hung up the phone. She stood silent in the courtyard for a few minutes, pulling herself together. They'd ended the conversation on a more peaceful note, even though Stella was still upset.

Despite her brave front with Stella, the conversation had taken a lot out of her. She felt as though she'd been run over by a dump truck after all the ups and downs of the past few days. Between the DNA comparison results, Cathy's claims to ownership of the cafe, and the marriage of convenience with Ryan, she could really use a day or two of rest. She needed to catch up on some sleep and maybe binge-watch a romantic comedy series. Then again, a few good books would probably do the trick. She'd stop at the bookstore on the way home from work.

Chapter Thirty-Nine

NINETEEN YEARS AGO

The letter fell to the desk and Helen left it there, her gaze shifting from the words on the page to the photos that spilled out of the envelope behind it. The images depicted a young girl with blonde curls that clung down her back. She wore a swimsuit with a rash-shirt and squinted into the bright sun, a gap-toothed smile lighting up her tanned face.

Helen's heart skipped a beat. It was Matilda, her daughter. The one she would never get a chance to raise. She looked happy. That was enough.

Her throat tightened and a sob worked its way out. She couldn't look away. She traced the outline of the little girl's face with a fingertip, wishing she could hold her, hug her, hear all about her day at the beach. There were other photos too. One of a birthday cake with six candles and Matilda blowing them out with a stern expression on her face when it seemed one candle refused to be extinguished. Another was a photograph of Matilda riding a pony, her helmet lop-sided on top of her head, legs almost horizontal on either side of the rotund little animal's back.

Finally, she had her fill and looked away, searching for the words on the page that would tell her all about how Matilda was doing. They'd been doing this for four years now—exchanging letters. And the occasional phone call. Each updating the other about the children, their progress, what was new in their world. Helen sent letters and photographs to Matilda's family, and they sent them back to her. It was how they managed to keep putting one foot in front of the other after they'd all discovered the horrible truth about what had happened at the IVF clinic. A place they'd trusted with their most precious possession, their child. A group of doctors to whom they'd each given every ounce of belief they could muster on the difficult journey towards parenthood.

John and Daphne Berry, Matilda's parents, already had three other children. They were blessed beyond measure, in Helen's mind. But they'd wanted a fourth and yet couldn't get pregnant. They'd tried the clinics in Australia and then heard about one in Georgia with exceptional results. And that had been the fateful step that led them here. How the mishap had happened, no one could say.

The IVF clinic had closed ranks and muttered nonsensical things about contracts that were signed, culpability averted, and that there was no way of knowing what had happened. In other words, they didn't intend to own up to what they'd done. And none of them would ever find out for certain, but they knew enough. They knew, without a doubt, that they belonged to each other's biological families but had each been raised in happy homes on opposite sides of the world.

Just then, Julie trotted into the office, her long brown pigtails bouncing with each step. She stopped in front of the desk and held up her fingers. "You said four o'clock."

Helen's mind frantically searched for a promise she'd made. "Four o'clock to…"

"Go fishing at Auntie Rita's lake house. You said we'd take brownies. Remember?"

"Oh yeah, brownies. That's right. I baked them while you were at school. Get your swimsuit and we'll head over there now. I just have to put this away."

Julie loved fishing. But more than that, she loved Auntie Rita and the lake house. It was one of her happy places. Rita often babysat her, and the two of them had a very close relationship. It didn't hurt that Tyler was a little older and behaved like the big brother Julie had never had but always wanted. He baited her line, helped her reel in a catfish when it was too heavy for her to do it alone, and she followed him around like a happy little puppy. Sophie was younger, but Julie couldn't get enough of her. Sophie had short blonde hair and big soulful blue eyes. She thought the world of Julie, and when Tyler wasn't interested in playing big brother, Julie would engage in make-believe with Sophie for hours on end.

Helen was so grateful for Julie's cousins. She regretted that Julie didn't have any siblings. It was a lonely life for the little girl, with Helen working at the hospital so often. In the end, Rita had offered to pick her up from school each afternoon so that Helen could stop sending her to daycare, and Julie spent hours each day at the lake house with her aunt and cousins, baking, playing, swimming, and fishing. It was her favourite haunt. And Helen tried very hard not to take it personally that she preferred going there to their own suburban and very quiet home.

The truth was, she loved being at the lake house herself. So, she could hardly fault her daughter for it. The only thing she wished was that she could tell Rita the truth about what she'd discovered—the truth about her daughter, Matilda, who lived in a small beachside town called Kingscliff, thousands of miles across the ocean.

But she couldn't. It wouldn't change anything. It wouldn't help anyone. And it might impact the way Rita accepted and loved Julie. Helen doubted it would. She knew her sister was sincere in her love for Julie, and biology wouldn't change that. But she couldn't risk it. Rita meant so much to Julie. It wasn't worth taking the chance that the truth could irreversibly alter their relationship. It was selfish of her to want to talk about the situation—it would help her feel better to share it with someone else. But it wouldn't be what was best for Julie. They couldn't fix what'd been done. All she could do now was pretend it hadn't happened. And then watch from a distance as someone else raised her and Paul's precious child.

Chapter Forty

CURRENT DAY

The lake was lovely at night, the water inky black. It was silent when the motor was still, leaving only the gentle lapping of the lake around the boat's sides. Ryan's boat was sleek, with a centre console and space for a table with padded seating around it. Matilda sat, hunched over with one bent leg hugged to her chest, looking out across the water and revelling in the peacefulness it brought to her soul. Ryan threw the anchor over the side, then opened a cooler. He set several containers on the table, along with plastic wine glasses.

"I hope you're hungry," he said. "I made fried chicken and gravy."

"I'm famished," she said. "I spent the half of the day on the phone with my family members. They're calling all the time, wanting information about Julie and what I've learned, and asking me if I'm really, truly certain." She laughed and ran her fingers through her hair. "I think they're more wigged out by the whole situation than I am. I've known for a while there was something amiss."

"It'll take them some time to process," he said. "The story is a strange one, even for those of us on the outside of it." He handed her a glass of champagne and then held up his own. "To new beginnings."

She smiled. "Cheers."

They drank. She watched him out of the corner of her eye while pretending to be studying the lake shore. He was gorgeous. But it wasn't just about the way he looked There was a confidence, a comfort in his own skin, that she found appealing. She couldn't believe he was interested in her. She'd always seen herself as more of the frumpy, uncoordinated type who grew on a person over time. Perhaps that was why she'd expected so little of Cam and had accepted his lacklustre commitment to her. She hadn't seen herself as being worth more than that.

But now, with everything that'd happened in the past few months, she wanted more. Needed more than that. She felt she deserved to be loved well by a man who enjoyed spending time with her and wanted to know what she thought.

He spun to face her, then reached for her hand and held it in his. Tingles ran through her fingertips and up her arm. It was exciting to be so close to him. To be touching him. She leaned closer so that her shoulder pressed up against his arm.

"What are you doing for Fourth of July?" he asked.

"I don't have any plans. That's more than a month away."

"We could take the boat over to the other side of the lake —there's a restaurant that makes great burgers."

"That sounds good."

"They have fireworks too."

"Do you always make plans so far in advance?" She was teasing him, but she liked it. He was planning ahead.

"I'm making sure you're still going to be around in July." His thumb ran gently over hers.

"I'll be here."

"Good."

She gazed up at him, her eyes meeting his. It was hard to see his expression in the darkness, but his face looked kind. Familiar. She knew him. And he knew her. It had only been a few months, but already he was closer to her than Cam had been after two years. She trusted this man with her heart. She hadn't been ready to do that when he first spoke of it, but now she was ready. She knew who she was, where she came from. The truth had settled in her spirit until she was at peace. She might not need him for her visa any longer, but she wanted him. That was more than enough.

He leaned down, tenderly grazing her cheek with his knuckles, then cupped her cheek in one hand, not breaking eye contact. His smile faded and a passionate intensity filled his eyes. Her lips yielded to him as her posture softened against him. His kiss was soft and teasing, reminiscent of summers at the beach and the freshness of a field after rain. She kissed him back sweetly, ardently, as a tremor ran through her body.

He framed her face with his hands, his kiss becoming more urgent, his lips searching and seeking as though he needed more. She surrendered completely, her eyes squeezed shut and her heart racing. Finally, he drew back, looking deep into her now open eyes.

"Do you still feel the same way you did before?" he asked. "Because I don't want to push you into anything..."

"No, I don't," she said. "Everything has changed. I'm finally at ease with my life and who I am. I'm ready to move forward. And I want to do that with you."

He grinned, and with a little shake of his head, said. "When I first met you, I thought you were rude. Obnoxious even. But ever since that first moment when you fell on those slippery tiles, there was always something about you that drew me in. I found it infuriating for a while, it bothered me to be attracted to someone who seemed so opposite to me in every way. But it didn't take me long to realise I'd been completely wrong about you. You're the perfect compliment to me, the balance I need in my life. You make every day worth whatever it brings. You're the one I want to see when I'm tired and have had a hard day at work. Even living next door is too far away. You healed my wounded heart and gave me back a chance at life again."

Tears sprang onto her cheeks at his words. He kissed them away, then his lips found hers again and they kissed passionately and deeply.

Chapter Forty-One

One month later, Matilda had finished her shift at the cafe when Rita arrived. She'd recently had her surgery and had recovered well. Matilda was managing the cafe while she was out of action. Rita walked into the empty cafe looking a little pale but otherwise well.

"I have good news!" she said, eyes bright.

Matilda wiped down an empty table, then turned to greet her with a kiss on the cheek. "You're looking good today. What's the news?"

"My cousin, Cathy, has given up the legal challenge to the ownership of the cafe."

"She has?"

Rita nodded. "We came to an agreement."

"What's the agreement?" Matilda asked with trepidation. She hated to think of Cathy owning part of the cafe. It was Rita's. Everything about it spoke of her taste, her work ethic, her passion for the place.

"I agreed to let her help manage the place for half of each week. With the condition that if it didn't work, she could be fired."

Matilda gaped. "You're going to let Cathy into the Honeysuckle Cafe? She'll ruin it."

"We had a good conversation. I think she'll behave herself. Anyway, if she doesn't, she knows what the consequences will be. And she gets no ownership stake in the place. At least, not yet, anyway."

Matilda decided not to ask about that. "It's your call. If that's what you want, I support you."

Rita huffed. "I don't want you stuck here. You're young and in love. You have a career. You've been so helpful to me while I've needed it, but you should forge a life of your own."

"I like it here," Matilda protested.

"I know you do." Rita smiled at her. "And you're a doll for saying that. But I don't want to tie you down. Cathy seems determined to be part of the cafe. And who am I to stop her? She has a point—her father was part owner. And let's be honest, I'm struggling to keep this place going on my own with all the health scares I've had lately. It might be nice to have some more help."

"I'm worried she'll just bring more stress into your life."

"Pshaw! I can handle Cathy. I've dealt with her my whole life. What I really want to talk about is what's going on with you and Ryan?"

The two of them sat down. Matilda dropped the cleaning cloth on the table. "Well, I'm not sure what to say. Things are great. As you know—I live with you." She laughed.

Rita shrugged. "I know you're out on dates with him several nights a week, and you visit his house every other night. But I want to know—is it serious?"

"That's a little personal, isn't it?"

Rita grunted. "I'm beyond that, honey. I've had a major surgery, my ticker is acting up, and I don't know how long I'll be around. You've got to give me something to live for."

Matilda rolled her eyes. "You sure are milking this thing..."

"For all it's worth." Rita's eyes sparkled.

Matilda sighed. "Okay, yes, we're serious."

"You're in love?"

"Absolutely." Matilda sighed again, this time in resignation. She could no longer ignore her heart. It'd taken her somewhere she hadn't expected. She'd fully believed she'd be back home in Brisbane by now, but between Rita's health issues and dating Ryan, it looked as though she wouldn't be back there for a while.

Rita clapped her hands together. "Awesome. I love me some romance. And I've been hoping someone would scoop Ryan up for years. He's such a good man."

"I agree, he is. And I'm glad no one else scooped him."

"So, you're staying here in Georgia?"

"For now."

"Doesn't your family miss you?"

"They do, but they understand. It's time for me to have my own adventure."

"Well, honey, I'm glad your adventure brought you here. And I hope you stay a while."

THE END

Also by Lilly Mirren

WOMEN'S FICTION

THE SUNSHINE SERIES

The Sunshine Potluck Society

Four friends start a monthly potluck brunch when their lives begin to unravel.

Sunshine Reservations

An old bed and breakfast by the beach and a restaurant that was burned to the ground, give Gwen an opportunity to start afresh after divorce.

The Summer Pact

When Beth Prince was thirteen years old she met a boy on New Year's Eve at Sunshine Beach. They talked all night and when the sun rose they vowed that they'd meet back at the same place in 15 years.

A Sunshine Christmas

Maree Houston's ex-husband is back in Sunshine for

Christmas and she quickly discovers that a stolen kiss could ruin everything. Including her big secret.

CORAL ISLAND SERIES

The Island

After twenty five years of marriage and decades caring for her two children, on the evening of their vow renewal, her husband shocks her with the news that he's leaving her.

The Beach Cottage

Beatrice is speechless. It's something she never expected — a secret daughter. She and Aidan have only just renewed their romance, after decades apart, and he never mentioned a child. Did he know she existed?

The Blue Shoal Inn

Taya's inn is in trouble. Her father has built a fancy new resort in Blue Shoal and hired a handsome stranger to manage it. When the stranger offers to buy her inn and merge it with the resort, she wants to hate him but when he rescues a stray dog her feelings for him change.

Island Weddings

Charmaine moves to Coral Island and lands a job working at a local florist shop. It seems as though the entire island has caught wedding fever, with weddings planned every weekend. It's a good opportunity for her to get to know the locals, but what she doesn't expect is to be thrown into the middle of a family drama.

The Island Bookshop

Evie's book club friends are the people in the world she relies on most. But when one of the newer members finds herself confronted with her past, the rest of the club will do what they can to help, endangering the existence of the bookshop without realising it.

An Island Reunion

It's been thirty five years since the friends graduated from Coral Island State Primary School and the class is returning to the island to celebrate.

THE WARATAH INN SERIES

The Waratah Inn

Wrested back to Cabarita Beach by her grandmother's sudden death, Kate Summer discovers a mystery buried in the past that changes everything.

One Summer in Italy

Reeda leaves the Waratah Inn and returns to Sydney, her husband, and her thriving interior design business, only to find her marriage in tatters. She's lost sight of what she wants in life and can't recognise the person she's become.

The Summer Sisters

Set against the golden sands and crystal clear waters of Cabarita Beach three sisters inherit an inn and discover a mystery about their grandmother's past that changes everything they thought they knew about their family...

Christmas at The Waratah Inn

Liz Cranwell is divorced and alone at Christmas. When her friends convince her to holiday at The Waratah Inn, she's dreading her first Christmas on her own. Instead she discovers that strangers can be the balm to heal the wounds of a lonely heart in this heartwarming Christmas story.

EMERALD COVE SERIES

Cottage on Oceanview Lane

When a renowned book editor returns to her roots, she rediscovers her strength & her passion in this heartwarming novel.

Seaside Manor Bed & Breakfast

The Seaside Manor Bed and Breakfast has been an institution in Emerald Cove for as long as anyone can remember. But things are changing and Diana is nervous about what the future might hold for her and her husband, not to mention the historic business.

Bungalow on Pelican Way

Moving to the Cove gave Rebecca De Vries a place to hide from her abusive ex. Now that he's in jail, she can get back to living her life as a police officer in her adopted hometown working alongside her intractable but very attractive boss, Franklin.

Chalet on Cliffside Drive

At forty-four years of age, Ben Silver thought he'd never find love. When he moves to Emerald Cove, he does it to support his birth mother, Diana, after her husband's sudden death. But then he meets Vicky.

An Emerald Cove Christmas

The Flannigan family has been through a lot together. They've grown and changed over the years and now have a blended and extended family that doesn't always see eye to eye. But this Christmas they'll learn that love can overcome all of the pain and differences of the past in this inspiring Christmas tale.

MYSTERIES

White Picket Lies

Fighting the demons of her past Toni finds herself in the midst of a second marriage breakdown at forty seven years of age. She struggles to keep depression at bay while doing her best to raise a wayward teenaged son and uncover the identity of the killer.

In this small town investigation, it's only a matter of time until friends and neighbours turn on each other.

About the Author

Lilly Mirren is an Amazon top 20, Audible top 15 and *USA Today* Bestselling author who has sold over two million copies of her books worldwide. She lives in Brisbane, Australia with her husband and three children.

Her books combine heartwarming storylines with realistic characters readers see as friends.

Her debut series, *The Waratah Inn*, set in the delightful Cabarita Beach, hit the *USA Today* Bestseller list and since then, has touched the hearts of hundreds of thousands of readers across the globe.

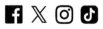

Printed in Great Britain
by Amazon